Hello Christy. Thank you for helping
me through my mid-terms.
Sometimes you make me feel like
it's okay to wake up
entirely disoriented.

PLEASE DON'T LEAVE ME

stories

JARET FERRATUSCO

(BrownpaperpublishinG)

First Printing

ISBN: 978-1-43484-827-7

Cover photograph: Jaret Ferratusco
Author Photograph: Amanda Boekhout

Published By Brown Paper Publishing

www.brownpaperpublishing.net
www.predicatemag.com
www.corpseonpumpkin.com

Printed in the United States of America

For George Ottawa,
wherever you went,
wherever you are.

CONTENTS

PLEASE DON'T
LEAVE ME

forward

AND I WOULD WATCH HER hunched over, with her back bent, skittering in jagged motions through thickets, trying to grasp its tail. I liked the way the muted sunlight played with her hair and skin and wished we'd not been burned so badly in that fire. Because we stood out, even here in the middle of nowhere. She would stand up straight, arms set at her sides in the drawing fashion of a gunslinger at the ready, looking to either side of the deep paw prints for any sense of movement. I kept falling in love over and over again, each time the whites of her eyes changed sides, rhythmically roving from side to side, hypnotizing. Then she would press on slowly, hunched over, with me not so far behind, smiling at the crunching of leaves. Following her following a rabbit. I tripped over a large, damp log, coming face first into a very well-manicured pile of leaves, raked tall and neat. When I pulled myself up again, she was sitting in front of me, balanced on both her knees, brushing leaves and dirt from a pale green t-shirt with a smallish pocket in the front. I sat up on my knees, too. And we stayed there, looking at each other as rabbits occasionally braved rustling paths through the now demolished pile of leaves.

A crumpled corpse lying on its back further up, face-up, head tilted backward, downhill, on a light slope, toes toward the sky, caught my attention. The head was split open at the side and one of the arms was pulled backward, out of its socket, and wrapped around the waist – an uncomfortable position, indeed. What I'd earlier taken for a mountain peak, from so far away, had turned out to be, the closer I got to it, that cracked, protruding elbow. Old blood and stretched skin marred the expression on its face, but I could make out tiny little teeth bent forward, pushed from a tiny rip in the flesh that might once have been a gentle mouth, as though a large object had been stuffed into the victim's face and decidedly ripped out again, leaving behind a limp handful of flesh and stuff and shattered things. She leaned back and the sunlight shone better on the drawing in the dirt and on her. And God she was beautiful. Her hair and clothes so black, skin so white, lips so red. The corpse was very graceful in its stillness. It complemented her as she examined it, and complemented how alone we were out here. It was thin and flowing, its death scrawled before our eyes by a ghost not yet pleased with itself, scribbling nuances in the bent body as the sun worked its way over the woods, and as elegant as it was ghastly, we hovered over the body in awe. Truly I marveled at it. I closed my eyes and held the picture in my head, which made me spin a little on the inside. When I opened them again, it was the same picture, only more vivid, and certain, and I was in love with never wanting to stand up again to leave this rare exception to every rule before me.

But nothing lasts forever.

an angel
points, angrily

A girl walks by in a gray dress, hugging her umbrella so tight over the back of her head that she's not keeping the torrents from soaking off the top of the umbrella straight down into her low top shoes. Not wearing any socks, shivering and slipping around inside her sneakers with every awkward step down the sidewalk, I begin to wonder if this kind of thing means I should close my eyes and not watch anything being done by anyone around me, until it's time to go home.

The rain, despite it's awkward welcome in sunlit warmth, it poured down from the sky like the stars had all of a sudden accepted this planet's gravity, too, tugging down all of limitless space, the whole outspoken black scope of it reeling in. Not even the common ant, tinier than a granule of dirt, could wander with any success between the drops of this violent rain as it hammered every inch of space outside the drug store my father waited in line inside of, for pills that would presumably -or so I eavesdropped his doctor relating- make him okay with the fact that my mother was dead at age thirty-five, some eight or nine years into a marriage supposedly made in Heaven.

The way it sounds like a war outside on the walkway, as heavy as the rain is, I'm surprised that I don't feel it much, and it's really only a slightly tougher glass window to see through, for between even the sheaths of waterfall torrents chasing the windows of the drugstore from top to bottom like a wavy segue into a dream, I could still see him as good as I would have wanted to. Jittery and sweating in a wrinkled suit, himself only slightly wet from the drizzle that had just begun to fall as we approached the front door to the place, my father stood wringing his hands nervously.

When I said to him 'I'll wait outside, papa' he'd only slightly noticed me. A disconnected sigh and accompanying nod bowed in like crashing rafters from the top of his head until his chin touched the sternum, like the last action he would be capable of until he too was dead, but though filled with love, at this point it was -and I actually felt okay with this despite not having a fraction of a clue why- simply retaliation to outside forces breaking into his private inferno of loss, the regrets of love, and the love of his life supposedly, in alternate worlds, or presumably, rather, regretting the day such love was founded. Sometimes you get the hint easily, and when my father looked at me in the way he did, I understood instantly that my mother -his wife- was a loss neither of us were at the gates yet of understanding.

But that's a different thing. My father's understanding of it, that is.

For me, a chiseled stalagmite standing in the pulverizing rain, years frozen, it was an entirely different story. I watched my father stand grimly in line like a homeless person waiting out his barking stomach's chance for a morning's breakfast at a struggling soup kitchen. Through the watershed and the small rainbows sparkling in the mist, I could see his stomach grumbling justly so, in absolute need of something. It was a very hungry need that affected his posture, and watching this, not fully comprehending this first time I'd ever witnessed my father queue for counsel but kind of understanding it as a matter of acute loss, I tried to weigh my options.

Possibly, I could be in waiting for a living zombie. My friend Chesney, a few years ago, his father was struck by a milk delivery truck on 42nd street, right in front of the school. We kind of saw it happen, Chesney and I. Most of it seemed entirely unreal to me, and afterward, seeing the look on my friend's face, I think it was far too much for him to really comprehend either. The initial contact where my friend's dad came under the scrutiny of the truck's steaming grill was as momentous and ear-cracking as an opening fire gunshot starting a race: The heads turning, all over the playing fields of the kid-littered streets, as every last set of eyes targeted in on the body at exactly the same time, this is when it started to resemble some kind of fantasy race to me instead of Chesney's father being killed, and that was when the Race started. I could feel the heart vacate my chest and I didn't feel like *I* was alive anymore either. It continued like this, racing through the seconds but forming each detail slowly. The first onlooker's fist to shoot out and pop an index finger in the direction of the body flying like a dart through the air, that was first place winner in the race. People screamed and it sounded like cheers. When Chesney's father's dead, dummy-like body tried to find peace in the windshield of an on-coming station wagon twenty feet off but only bounced off and hit the front of the milk truck a second time, and some kid who happened to be standing directly next to me squealed which such a pitch it was like a referee's whistle, he unwittingly landed second place. It was scoring points to notice the horror first even though everyone was seeing the same thing. Chesney's father came to a halt, finally—unbelievably—inside the back-lit early-morning marquee of Rally Jameson Elementary's roadside welcoming sign, pitching stick-on letters every which way to Hell and back. I couldn't believe if what I had seen was real. My pulse ran in pursuit of my darting eyes. And then I looked to my side, at the slack, upright pile of flesh I used to have a really good time with a lot; my friend Chesney. From then on, after witnessing this, he became a mute.

That's what my father looked like at this point; as Chesney has since the accident.

Watching from outside as my father began what I perceived to be a new march into the non-living years of the rest of his life, I didn't actually know at that point exactly how my mother had died, to begin with. Only that she was gone and the death itself was supposedly Unmentionable and Kind Of Confusing. But the way my father's eyes seemed to hold their ground staring at all times directly in front of him – *just like Chesney after his own father's deat*h – I had the distinct feeling that my father knew a little more than he was telling me when he said a few nights previous to the funeral that '*What you see is what you get.*'

But let's think about this a moment. My father was a pilot for a major airline. Weighing things out – scrutinizing the rings of the seed's tree – he *never* allowed my mother and I to fly anywhere on a plane, ever, citing reasons that to me, back then, seemed unerringly daydreamed and rather ominously incredulous. One night – which became the first of many – I heard him ranting to my mother – long past my intended bedtime – that demons were common on plane flights – hear my mother weep to herself silently – hanging about on the wings for the thrill of so closely Heavenward a flight, supposedly taunting God with the murder of his children. My mother, I do remember, cried herself into vast oceans of tears after these stories spilled from my father's pale, rye-chapped lips following most of his many days-long haunts in the clouds. Sometimes during breakfast she'd ask if I knew of any particulars concerning Papa's travels that she didn't know I knew about. And even that young, her questioning seemed like loaded interrogations stacked with volume upon volume of immeasurable grief. So being a good kid each time, returning her worried look with one I thought would calm her fears with my boyish innocence, I simply played the dumb little boy, proclaiming with an unnatural eagerness and excitement I didn't really comprehend the origins of '*Papa's a human bird!*'

What does a bird's brain weigh? Half a feather? I must have seemed like a zombie myself. My mother cried softly sometimes after asking me this.

But what does a kid do? At that age, when life's merely a momentous lily pad fostered within a fenced yard during the daytime and the numbered walls of the house as night fell, he has only his parents to dictate to him the reality of his surroundings. And at that point in my life, admittedly, I was still struggling with brutal dreams that plagued me night after night, of short-tempered reindeer stomping to death neighborhood children during Christmastime. In newly collected exchange, as it were, for *countless* decades of unpaid-for toys delivered in the dark without a single thank-you from anybody, on all those sorrowful Christmas mornings.

Sometimes I would just stare at my mother and smile, and after a fashion – this was before her death – she'd cry.

horse and
pig shadow

'Let's see you make something of yourself' my brother taunted, pushing me ever so lightly at the shoulders, mockingly, so that whenever I took a step back, despite his not pushing me all that hard, I still tripped a little. 'I dare you,' he said, laughing.

With all the focus narrowed down to needle points and nowhere to retreat to escape this, his voice felt somehow separated from his face; a ghost recording coming from the picture frame my brother was centered in. Leering at me, his face seemed to blur a little, piling transparent pictures over solid ones to form a mean, provoking flip-book I really didn't want to be flipping. And suddenly all the sound around us was gone, leaving just that of my brother's taunts and his jeers to ring and echo in the barber shop, bouncing off stainless steel scissors and wiped down mirrors. When the laughter settled some, the sound from his lips quieted down into a sullen hiss.

Today, in the absence of his regular, more qualified friends, my brother Gill hauled me along to the barber shop to drink some soda pop and observe the high school girls who walked by the outside window, down the sidewalk into the infamy of memory. There was no point to it, really, especially being that we were positioned behind a wall of glass and reflections and couldn't holler or whistle at the girls to get their attention, but I felt like I was king of the world there, with my older brother. Just two neighborhood roustabouts with nothing better to do than cause a scene.

There really wasn't much of a scene to cause, however. Nevertheless, I think we were doing fine at it.

My brother was a respected thief amongst the neighborhood kids. In the shop, I kept an admiring eye on him around the barber's combs, hoping to catch one disappear into his pocket so that later, when he was outside combing his hair, I'd know defiance, and somehow it would make me stronger and a little less hesitant to do the same. But all the while that I suspected Gill had a pocketful of new possessions, I didn't see a thing, which made me feel like I was somehow out of the loop.

Even though it was often a spoken rule made plainly apparent that my presence could only be tolerated on days like this for loss of available friends from his own grade hall at school, I still had a great time going out with Gill. Beside the fact that I admired him unfailingly, girls liked him as well; though mother won't let me alone with girls, she'd never said a word about Gill's constant and sometimes questionable company of them. In that respect as well as countless others, being with Gill made me feel like I wasn't a child anymore, like I could breath out loud without someone on my back about it. And I always took it that since Gill was a lot older, he was allowed that much more freedom, but oft times – or every chance he got, really – Gill would say it was more a matter of mother liking him a lot better. I'd swallow that kind of talk with strenuous efforts made to forget about it, calling up that rebellious look in his eye and trying to emulate it without exactly copying it.

About half an hour ago, the neighborhood dart-board, Mare, had burst into the barber shop, screaming like she'd been pushed against a hot stove, telling us all she'd just found a dead body in the field on Ally Caimber's farm.

Both grotesque and wildly imaginative, instantly I'd started at her descriptions, reeling back as though from a fright on the picture show screen. But Gill and even Billy Wells, the proprietor of the shop, only laughed and shrugged her off. People do this a lot around Mare because she's wholly seventeen years of age if not eighteen, she's abnormally slow, her eyes aren't always looking at the same thing at the same time, she drools and cannot spell her own name to save her life. The other kids call her Night Mare. She doesn't get it at all.

Mare's father drinks a lot and I've seen him tip-toe up behind her, strike the poor girl in the back of the head and then dash like a carnival clown – all bumbling steps with drunken, unsure footing – to hide behind the car in the drive port; twice I've witnessed this, which makes me think it happens a hell of a lot more when nobody's around to see it. She'll turn around, too slow to catch him for he'll have dipped behind that car, or a tree, and she gets scared and runs off crying, throwing her arms up and groping at the air like she's trying to climb an invisible ladder. I've never really been the one to laugh at her much, and I'd certainly not wanted to start now, especially when she was so wracked up telling us about a discarded cadaver only a quarter of a mile away from my house.

Gill slapped the back of my head for something like the third time and asked 'What's the matter, Kevin? Scared?'

A flash-lit scene of Mare getting slapped in the back of the head by her father popped into my head like the correct answer on the screen of a television game show, complete with an old man pasty and made up under manicured hair, stiff make-up covering the lines in his face and dressed hauntingly mannequin-like in a shiny suit, goading the studio audience into cheering, pointing to me from across the stage to quip 'That is correct! You are scared!'

I was undoubtedly scared, yes. But the hell if I were going to say or show as much to Gill. So with a good intake of air, I ran through it in my head a few times, then exhaled and barked out my line. Exactly what Gill had dared me to say to her: 'Go fucking home,' I cried, sounding more helpless than I think Mare felt.

For the second time, all motion, all sound drained. Left menacingly, there was just the sour, lingering atmosphere created by what I'd blurted out, but not echoing with a boom like Gill's voice might have. I was thunderous, sure, but somehow sadly confined. The syllables in the air stopped short, trapped behind jailhouse bars. When Gill shouts, people listen up, but coming from my mouth, and even before I'd finished saying it, all I felt was embarrassment. It sounded so petty.

When an eternity had passed in silence, my brother stepped briskly out of the way as Billy Wells lunged toward me and smacked me in the side of the head a lot harder than Gill just had. He twisted my arm, bending down into my face, with a few small, black plastic combs slipping from his vest pocket, clattering to the floor. 'Now you apologize to Mare, Kevin Henry, or I'll smack you so hard in the ass your poor mother will be able to hear it all the way from your home.'

Gill stood behind the old barber and snickered at me while my face grew red and just as I'd been ordered to, taking orders like usual, I promptly apologized to Mare. The truth is, I really was sorrier than just the words could have offered the girl – who by now was crying and making her way back toward the front door – but I still couldn't back down in front of my brother. For some reason, I needed to prove myself today. So I stood there, trying my best to organize a sneer on my face I thought might look mutinous. In my mind, I was hoping to lead the way into a flying parade of middle fingers and curse words, helming the new revolution against barbers and helpless little girls.

But I was alone in that misshapen crusade. Gill was propped up against the front door with his head down, leaving me in the spotlight to take any and all blame coming our way.

My big heroic finale never came, either. Merely grumbling softly to himself, shaking his head sadly, Billy Wells collected his plastic combs, tucked them neatly back into the pocket of his vest and ordered Gill and I to leave his shop at once, warning that if we didn't go straight home he'd call our mother.

Aside from still being horribly embarrassed and disappointed in myself for what I'd done to the vulnerable and simple girl, privately I was also very happy that Billy had not only yelled at me for what I'd said, but also he'd scolded my brother too, for it was Gill who'd wanted so badly for me to say it anyhow, so we both deserved it. Pathetically, in another way entirely, it served to make me more like Gill's accomplice rather than simply being his younger brother, and the small part of me that I wished to expand reveled in it. Defeated – but defeated together –I was now part of the same snide goings-on one of the other boys in the higher grade halls were always up to. When we both suffered the same punishment I didn't feel so much like I'd just been tagging along anymore. I guess being mean feels a lot better when people are in on it with you.

We muttered 'Yes, sir' in unison and left. Once out in the street, however, Gill spat at a telephone pole. His spittle ran down the face of a hand-posted sign detailing the advantages of purchasing a used tractor. The ink on the sign was still somewhat fresh and puddled a little as the spit ran out of energy to run. 'The fuck if I'm gonna let an old man tell me that I have to go home,' Gill said to the signpost.

'Yeah,' I spat too. 'He can't tell us what to do.'

And for the love of God, Gill smacked me again, this time even harder. 'You best shut your trap, Kevin. It's that big mouth of yours got us into this in the first place. And if that old bastard actually calls mother, I'm telling her everything you said.'

After that, we mostly walked home in silence.

Or rather, I followed his lead, three steps behind and feeling a hundred more beside.

Despite Gill's rebuke against listening to the barber's orders, home was indeed our next destination. We walked the Arches Road on the way back, which wound all kinds of ways like a lazy snake around the woods, seemingly going nowhere. Our house was a lot like nowhere, in any case. So it led in the right direction, it seemed. The street itself was mostly paved by dirt, but is here and there flaked by what appeared to be aborted attempts at tar being put down. It also passes by Allen Emmen Caimber's farm, whose corn field is where all the older kids go to smoke and drink beer they've stolen or paid someone even older to buy for them. They always say Caimber's field is off limits to kids like me—the older ones say this, anyway. They try to scare me with ghost stories and stuff like that.

But I get the feeling most that do go there don't go too deep into it either.

Before I was born, Allen Emmen Caimber shot his wife in the head. Astonishingly, though her face wasn't so much to look at anymore, she survived the attack and so, since he wasn't technically a murderer, he was released from jail only six years later. And to this day they both still live in that house, though nobody hardly ever sees them. Sometimes they come to church. Mostly they don't.

Over the bank of the hill, from where we walked, the corn field looked healthy, almost pleasant.

But up close, it smelled like rotting vegetables and looked like a tornado had battered it twice or more. About every three or four years Caimber will take care of that field, but generally it's just him needlessly planting and then staunchly neglecting. So far as anyone knows, the old man doesn't make money on that farm at all, and he doesn't quite sell anything off the land – at least to anybody in town. So considering that and the fact he lives with a wife he shot in the head, people regard him as crazy and nobody bothers with the Caimber farm much.

'You think Mare really saw a dead body in that field, Gill?'

To this my brother laughed menacingly. 'You'd have to be pretty fucking stupid to believe a word Mare says. Almost as crazy as that old bastard Caimber. What's a dead body doing on a fucking farm?'

I thought about this for a moment. 'Yeah, but isn't that the point? Caimber's crazy. He shot his wife. Who's to say there isn't someone else he's tried to kill? Or has killed?'

'Well for starters, Kevin, that old man shot his wife because she was out in the field one night and he thought it was a bandit come for the corn. He's crazy, sure, but he didn't try to kill his own wife on purpose. He just aimed in the dark and fired is all. Defending his property like anybody would.'

I stopped walking. 'So you don't think Caimber's crazy?'

'No. He's crazy, all right. Spent six years in jail. Wouldn't you be crazy after that?'

Thinking harder on it, wondering why the farmer wouldn't just as soon shoot someone else in his field if he'd done it once already, I remembered that Caimber had actually shot his wife while she was sleeping in bed, not out in a field. Either Gill was confused on rumors, or he was lying just to get a rise out of me, figuring I'd try to correct him and just give him another chance to make something else up. Rather than give in to it, I dropped that part of the subject, choosing to ignore any traps he may be setting me up for in the timeless process of amusing himself.

But I couldn't let the matter of the body rest. 'So what if Mare really saw a dead body?'

'You're an idiot, Kevin.'

'But what if it's true? What if it *is* Mrs. Caimber again?'

'You're an idiot, Kevin.'

'Mare's not that dumb, and you know she goes out walking in fields all the time. Why on earth would she lie about something like that?'

'You're an idiot, Kevin.'

Just like that. Gill was absolutely dead set on disregarding anything I said, yet goading me to say something more so he wouldn't run out of ways to tell me to shut up. His complete dismissal of me like this was infuriating. No matter how much I stood up for him even though he was so much of an asshole and treated me always with as much regard as anyone would give to a bag of garbage, Gill always found a way to stuff it right back into my mouth until I choked on it. Sooner or later I would have to say something about it, and as mad as I was, I wanted it to be sooner.

As I figured it, I needed to stand up somehow. Right here, I had my chance to give him every rotten thing he'd ever done to me right back in his face, I was so sick of him. I'm *not* an idiot, I kept telling myself. My body trembled as I sought inside whatever it took for me to strike him right in the face, but Gill saw it coming and I winced because he looked like he was going to hit me first, and he laughed and took off down the road faster than I could walk. And then it came to me to call his bluff. Having missed my chance to say it before when we were looking right at one another, I just yelled it out 'Well I think you're just scared to see what's really out there!'

Gill stopped running, slowly turning around to face me; really slow. Then he started walking back along the grassy dirt road toward me.

'You think I'm scared of a fucking field? Or a fucking corn field because of a retarded girl older than me who can't cross the road without holding her grandmother's withered hand?'

'Yes. I think you're scared.'

The next thing I knew I was bleeding from the nose and Gill was dragging me over deep, chaotic dirt paths in Caimber's field where the old man used to ride the tractor back and forth for hours on end, in circles. He dragged me over the tracks and into the corn stalks.

Pressing his fingers hard into my soft muscle, he twisted my arm around his fist like it was a bundle of rope and just kept pulling until I actually started to cry. Overjoyed at my whimpering, he took this opportunity to spit more names at me and made to punch me again. His fist cocked back, silhouetted by the orange sun behind him, and I winced just like before, so he laughed at me even harder, lightly slapping me on the face while he tugged. 'You're gonna see a dead body now! he starting screaming into my face. 'We're gonna see a dead body now!'

Rotten corn stalks eclipsing the sun above us, taller than trees. They crawled across the immediate sky, reaching out like the hulking corpses of scarecrows. Underbrush and spider webs caught on my face as he dragged me effortlessly through dry, musty clumps of weeds and soft, moldering oranges caked in the dirt, and when I tried to get a grip on a corn stalk it only fell apart, unable to keep itself together in my hands. Underfoot, twigs crackled, dead corn rustling. Gill stopped laughing so much because of the dead vegetable matter getting caught in his mouth as the rushing stalks whipped at us. He spat at the weeds as he pulled me.

I twisted in his grip while he just grunted and pulled harder with each outcry.

Then, just as abruptly as this tug of war had begun, it now ended. And with as much violence, too. He pushed me face down to the ground, rubbing my face against grass and dirt.

I was so embarrassed I could barely get up, but I gave it a good try, just to avoid anything else coming at my face from my asshole brother. I was so fed up with Gill I wanted to tear him to pieces. The well of violence rising in me was molten, searing my veins as my face shook. All I'd ever wanted to do was gain his acceptance; the cool kid, the one all the girls liked. But really, what the fuck was that worth if all he could do to get his kicks was bully a small shit like me who looked up to him for it? The older brother I idolized was, in fact, just a regular loser. He was a worthless, no good failure and could only ever end up as some dirty farmhand if he possibly managed to stay out of jail past eighteen. Looking him up and down, the embarrassment I'd been made to feel all day gained a thousand more burning degrees. My fist-beaten envy of him was now effectively erased. And I felt sick I'd ever looked up to him, the realization of it making my blood boil hotter.

Just as always he would until the end of time, he dragged me along with him today just to put me down. I was Gill's crutch, in a way, helping him walk by, physically becoming the bricks underneath his sneakers. Makes me break a slow girl's heart, gets me hit by a barber and sent home, punches me in the nose and mouth, kicks the shit out of me, and then pushes me down into filthy weeds. My fists curled into rocks.

All I wanted to do at that moment was jump up on my own two feet and punch him right in the mouth, splitting the lips away from his cracked teeth and then reaching in with both hands to tear his goddamned jaw out.

The train wreck anger provided me with a little extra strength, and I made it to my feet. Pulling myself up, I spit blood, with husks of corn stalks alternately slumped and hovering around my head like gray ghosts decayed in the breeze; the wind whistling through their bodies was a cold sound, making me shiver as I stretched then re-knotted my fists.

Gill standing taller than I, his lips stretched tight in a lopsided grin. The fucker was waiting for it; he wanted it; all crooked teeth in that shit-eating mouth. I'd give him a mouthful if my life depended upon it. Strong jaw, but not tough enough to stop me from breaking through it. My fists pulsed, squeezed white. Still raising myself up, I stared hard at him, imagining my fist lodged in his skull, his eyes popped out from the pressure.

'Well, where's the fucking body, Kevin? Huh?'

The blood in my arms and fists was a volcano now, scorching the inside of my chest, ready to shoot from my mouth in a geyser and torch the whole field.

'Well where's the fucking dead body, you piece of shit?' Now his fists were up too, ready for it. 'Come on *Kevin*! Where's the body?' He was laughing so hard I could have cried.

But . . . standing up to my full height, taking in full view the sight before my eyes, my legs and arms suddenly didn't feel so strong anymore. My fists lost the tension, the tightness relaxing as the frozen knots loosened.

Standing up to my full height, I shrunk a little again, and my body went cold and numb with what I was seeing behind Gill.

My fists disintegrated into the air like water molecules, so I let them completely loose and my fingers relaxed into a semi curl. With sweat turning to ice water on my forehead and down my back, I lifted a trembling finger at Gill, then more to the right, behind him. My arm stood straight out as I pointed, frozen. 'There,' I whispered ....

And there, with Gill moved a little out of the way as he turned, confused at what I pointed to, were a set of dirty bare feet poking out from the undergrowth at the edge of a worn path through the stalks.

The two of us stood there motionless, practically breathless. Inside my skin, the blood was curdling and my spine seemed to be shrinking. Suddenly, I didn't want to be anywhere near the field anymore. Instead, I wished Gill to take my arm again and drag me as far from Caimber's farm as violently as he'd brought me here. Just away, in any manner possible.

'What the hell is that?' Gill croaked, the fear in his voice something I'd never heard before.

'It's *feet*.'

We advanced only a few inches closer, gaining as much distance as ants would toward the bony white legs that disappeared into the underbrush of a falling orange tree.

Together, we edged closer, so slowly. Gill gasped loudly when we got close enough to discover that the body – that of a man – was completely naked. Turned slightly onto its side, the arms draped limply against the hips as if the carcass had wriggled its way into the bushes like a worm. And that's exactly how it looked, with a gutter of dirt gouged through the edge of the road at the end of its legs. The man's face was pressed hard into a grassy patch underneath the tree, like his head had been stomped on. There was no hair on his head, and upon closer inspection by Gill – who gasped again, coughing on his lack of breath – there were small patches of stubble, and deep, ragged cuts all over the scalp like the hair had not just been shaved but gutted by force.

Gill jumped back. His voice was now a whine, sounding more like me than even I did. 'Let's get the fuck out of here, Kevin.'

But I was not so inclined to move; half because my bones had turned to jelly at the same time I was stiff in my shoes, but also because this was the scariest looking man I had ever seen in my entire life.

He only barely looked human. More like a mannequin wrapped crudely in bleached skin. He was thin, to say the least, but all over his body were fatty, disproportioned deposits of flesh, like certain parts of him had refused to stop growing; on one shoulder there was a clump, and at both elbows, one near the small of back, and curdling the lower half of both legs so that he looked like he'd been wading through sour milk. By comparison, the skin at his feet was stretched tight over the bones of his toes and heels. Clumped up and scrunchy like a fat hound, but thick and waxy, his body looked partially rippled with tumors.

'Look at his skin, Gill.'

My brother shivered, nearly knocking me over as he shook closer to me. 'So? What about it?'

'He looks like rubber.'

Gill leaned in closer to the body, emitting a choking sound from deep in his throat that gurgled up to his mouth as he heaved, seeing that the man did look just like I'd observed, as if he'd been wrapped from head to toes in thick, waxy white rubber.

'He's probably . . . rotting, Kevin.'

But neither of us could smell death from this man. He was not breathing, which was evident, and the utter absence of color from his body spoke well of its status as a corpse, but the body appeared very far from rotting. Even further from rigor mortis, when Gill nudged the man's shoulders with his sneaker, the weight shifted and the body twisted more onto its back. Lifeless, but not stiff at all. If he was dead, he must have died only very shortly before poor Mare found him here. Which made all this even scarier. The both of us shot nervous glances down the path and between the cold stalks of corn.

'Fuck this. We're getting out of here.' Gill rested a trembling hand on my shoulder, but I struck it off. He said nothing, just kept staring at the body, his conviction dashed and temporarily forgotten as we continued to stare at the dead man.

'Let's pull it over,' I said.

'Are you *crazy*?' he yelled, looking at me as though I were mad.

'No. Let's drag it onto its back.'

Gill said nothing more, just stared intently at the corpse before us, his eyes wide and shiny as cup saucers. In a smaller, more fragile voice, he asked 'Do you think he might still be alive?'

'I don't know.'

Our words were well filled in between by bouts of silence that seemed to last years. Neither of us could take our eyes from the maybe-corpse for more than a few frantic seconds. And the chills running through my whole body barreled like trains down my bones, clicking over them like tracks. I didn't know why we should turn it around, only that we should. I wanted to see the face hidden behind that small, roundish head, the skin so tightly pulled that I could make out the shape of the skull underneath.

Not fighting what he was seeing – just mystified and scared – Gill did what I said and with our four hands on one of the dead man's arms, we pulled the corpse over.

This time Gill jumped back and screamed. The face was the worst of its amassed skin problem, absolutely fat with pale, sickly white flesh. To me, it looked like the body had simply been melting the whole time with its face down in the grass. The overlapping folds around the pits of the eyes had grown purple, as did the nose and around the mouth. But that mouth; it just wasn't right.

The man's mouth stretched, unbelievably, from one ear all the way to the other, wrapped in thick, bulbous lips as purple as the skin around the eyes, coming to fat little corners just under each ear. It looked like the most frightening mask I'd ever seen.

We stared, mortified and sick.

Then, the skin around the eyes drew visibly tighter with a sound like cloth being pulled beyond fabric's ability to stretch and when I could see the swelling purple lids appearing from under the fat over the eyes, horrifyingly, *they suddenly popped open.* My body froze up completely. Gill screamed and reached forward to pull me away from it, but I was stuck rigid.

The widening eyes under all that awful rubbery skin were small and sad, fastly welling with tears, and in the instant Gill's hands were on my arm, the body's massive jaw fell open and its mouth widened to display titanic white teeth sharper than broken glass and it lunged forward, taking half a bite out of my arm and with it, Gill's entire hand.

My brother and I both let go of the body like it was an exploding firecracker and all three of us—the awful non-corpse included—fell to the ground. It landed back on its face, exactly as if we had never touched it, unutterably motionless.

Gill picked himself up, flailing and flopping around like a rag doll. He set off running, slipping on putrid mounds of dead strawberries that were strewn everywhere, wildly screaming a racket so shrill it hurt my ears. The end of his wrist shot forth a fire hose stream of dark blood that fanned out and painted the dead orange trees above him and the sad gray dirt under his feet, leaving a broad, glistening trail as he disappeared off around the bend.

Propped up, in small turns gazing at the thick, dirtied trail of blood my brother had left behind him and then at the immobile naked white body, I fought to catch my breath.

Unable to move a muscle below my neck or piece together what just fucking happened, my eyes fell flat on this creature of some sort that attacked us, resigned to gaze at it. And the body, or whatever it was, lay there as perfectly still as when we'd first come across it. Half-sitting up, my arm torn open and seeping all kinds of matter and tissue with the rushing blood, I stared blankly, dizzy and nauseous, with no idea at all what to do. The world around me looked softer as I grew more and more lightheaded, the dizziness swirling in my head. My body started to shake with a chill I'd never felt the severity of before.

PLEASE DON'T LEAVE ME

fake scarecrow who
can't keep too
still

It was Halloween night, almost midnight, actually. There were still people everywhere. Some neighborhoods might have called it quits hours ago, but it was still young here tonight. The cable television had been out all week in the neighborhood, defying the odds that anyone might have lacked sleep. Since there was nothing to do at home, I had been taking walks all up and down the streets and in backyards and alleys and cold empty baseball diamonds, waiting for Halloween. I'd developed a mild cold from all this lurking about the neighborhood at such freezing wet hours of the night, seeing who had the best decorations or if anybody had motion detecting lights that didn't work. It was a shitty week, all around.

But tonight, it was perfect. Dry, breezy, mottled with the distant sounds of laughter and fake screams.

A bitter breeze swept the front yard where I was standing, rustling the trees, shaking down clouds of dead leaves to the grass, which were loudly trampled underfoot by an ocean's high tide of little fang-bearing werewolves, swaggering sailors, silvery shiny astronauts, lawyers with blood coming from their eyes, double-manned horses knocking into cars on the side of the street, and chainsaw wielding schizophrenics with curt laughter and shrewd candy-detecting practices, the wiliest of whom could be found on any really dark corner, running about, snatching pillow cases and double-lined shopping bags, plastic pumpkins filled with candy, or whatever else someone used to harvest their keep.

One little girl passed by me, wearing an angel outfit bearing huge white wings that extended violently from her back like massive claws, threatening to throw her balance; chalk white face paint and pitted black eye sockets smiled up at me. Grinning like she had rabies, the little girl angel with the deathly face bit my arm, on the way past. At this, her mother let loose a shrill cry of alarm, catching up to the girl, and she slapped the kid twice across the face, beseeching her coldly not to talk to strangers.

But the girl hadn't actually said a word to me, as it were. All she did was to bite me. A rabid angel can't be concerned with talking to strangers. Besides, the bite didn't hurt all that much.

From behind me came a simulated creaking sound swimming in radio-static as someone's front door opened. A booming voice loudly proclaimed 'Who Goes There?'

The answer he got was a muddy, unintelligibly high-pitched round of screams from the children on the porch. 'Trick Or Treat!' they shot back at him, off-key but stern.

The man with the booming voice cringed back with an overly sincere mock-retreat, bellowing 'Well then! I suppose I ought to make good on the treats, lest I be tricked!' This assertion was met with delirious laughter. A few seconds later, the group of kids came darting past me, still cheering, still at the peak of their years. For that moment, I was a mindless scarecrow, nestled in a conflagration of burning cornstalks, rustling, busy with intense, immediate motion. It was a really pretty night and every little tomahawk-wielding Indian or blank-faced, blank-hearted mime trying to escape an invisible box that scurried past me was a breath of fresh air, even though I wasn't really in the mood to take part in their revelry. Tonight, every movement I saw was obligatory, it seemed, and everything looked as right as things could be and as it should, but damnably, I felt extensively excluded. This was supposed to be the night anyone could let loose, but I felt like instead I was strapped up on a stake amidst a swarm of crows, not doing anything but waiting for one of them to perch on me. This was supposed to be a night for razor blades, apples, poison, knives, abduction, kissing, touching, laughing, screaming, robbing, smashing, destruction, for decadence and condoms littering the basement floor of some teenager's home, condoms littering the shorn grass behind a small tool shed in the dark part of someone's unfenced backyard.

It could be.

And for all I knew it probably was, for someone. It probably had to be, for at least two people, or maybe four, somewhere. Or some odd-numbered conflagration, like, five or something. But try as I might, I didn't hear any distant girls sighing out or any of their boys panting. Just little kings everywhere demanding recompense for the offences of third-grade knights. I didn't hear the rickety aluminum door of a backyard shed bending in from what new grasp people my age were supposed to be learning from this night; I was in the suddenly awkward generation, too old for free doorstep candy but young enough to speak up about it and maybe feel disassociated enough to want some kind of pity for it. What swam in the air with the icy winds was a steady current of children screaming 'Trick Or Treat' at the top of their raw lungs, and a sharp orchestra of winds slicing through my head with dry sonatas and movements, trees rustling and their leaves being crunched under size-four sneakers. I should have dressed as a ghost.

Occasionally, firecrackers rang out, popping like muskets and rifles. Or spooky songs played from dark windows on front lawns of newly-erected, small but ancient cemeteries of foam headstones and bright white, cotton candy cobwebs. I'd hear someone yell *Wait!* when the streetlights turned red, as a crowd of witches set marks to fly their brooms across the street. I'd observe frantic, wide-eyed parents in jeans and sweaters rushing to detain hasty rabbits erratically hopping too fast before oncoming cars flashing their brights.

'Can I help you, son?' was what I heard in that terrible fake booming voice from the porch, stomping heavily up behind me. It was like something you might hear coming from someone when you're browsing the shelves at a store. So I pulled myself together, stretched out my neck, balled my fists tight and left this stranger's lawn without giving him an answer. From behind me, the old man coughed, wheezing a bit, for the first time giving the lie to his forceful midnight presence by exhibiting a small slight in his health, and then the front door creaked shut with radio static, waiting in silence for the next batch of devils and pasty-faced angels. For another set of endless minutes with failing miserable body movements, to be woken from the slumber that will eventually kill it.

When I hit the sidewalk, I made an abrupt left and almost broke my forehead open against some lady trying to make a quick grab for her daughter, who had been running too fast. My whole head felt like it was reverberating, sounding off a bell only I could hear.

The little girl was dressed as a fairy. She had glittery silver wings reflecting glares from each passing streetlight or car. Her face was piled heavily with greasy streaks of white and silver paint, sprinkled with glitter. From the thighs up, she was all black polyester and glitter, waving a magic wand that was essentially, I guess, a twig. Black stockings and glittery shoes with little lights on them that sparkled when the soles touched the sidewalk. As I raised my pounding head to look at the mother, some heavyset kid shuffled past me, dressed like a fight just begging to happen, trying to cut my leg open with a cardboard sword. His costume was all cardboard, too, painted a lazy silver too drab to compliment the shitty costume. Bulging out in creases at the belly, he chuckled gracelessly. I felt bad for him, for some reason. A plastic helmet atop his head swung open at the face, which was pudgy and white with sweat, and the knight inside asked me 'Who Goes There?'

'Just a peasant,' I pleaded. 'Just a simple, honest peasant. Spare me, my Lord.'

The little boy inside the low-income armor giggled, and then relinquished his sword. 'As you were, then.'

His mother – trailing shortly behind him – smiled nervously at me. From inside my potato sack, she couldn't tell that I wasn't smiling back, but I nodded my head to her anyway, raising my arms in scarecrow position – which was also a little like a crucifixion pose – standing still. That worried look on her faced was replaced by relief, as she thought I probably lived here at the house whose lawn I was standing over, which, in fact, I didn't. How many of these parents out here tonight were hyperventilating every time their costumed little demons found themselves conversing with a complete stranger?

Conversing with a complete scarecrow, really.

My costume was beaten and old looking – realistic, at least – and I was half-way proud of it. I was dressed in ratty, muddied overalls and a reddish plaid long-sleeved shirt that looked as if it should have been retired decades ago. A straw hat hung at the dome of my skull, held over a potato sack with safety pins as splintered strands of straw poked out from under it or from tears in the sack around the neck. Two eyeholes were cut out so I could just barely see anything not directly in front of me. Straw fell from my shirtsleeves and from the cuffs of my pants. At first, I didn't think it needed confirmation, but earlier in the day I'd asked a friend what he thought I was. 'A filthy redneck farmer who probably got burned in the face a long time ago,' he'd said.

Someone else 'Some tattered chain-gang escapist from the Nineteen Thirties, hiding out in a haystack, trying to cover reputed scars across his face that could be recognized.' Too romantic, but at least not too stupid.

My father guessed that I was 'A fucking drop-out, ashamed to show his face even in his own house.' I looked myself over in the mirror, trying to see the same, coming to the conclusion that he was just drunk.

At twenty years of age, that I was – a drop-out, I mean. But I suppose being as old and spiritless as my father really was, he'd long forgotten that it was Halloween and who anyone really is during the other, altogether separate three hundred and sixty-four days of the year didn't apply. Besides, why would someone dress up and pretend just to be themselves? That's what boring family dinners were for.

But I thanked him, like always, and left home right before sundown, knocking back a few cans of beer I'd lifted from his Hidden Cooler in the cellar.

There's something to be said about a cloudy black sky and a raw off-white moon when there's a hundred kids running around blaring like sirens, high on chocolate, foaming at their mouths, delirious with the thought of being invincible little creatures. Almost nobody here out on the street is who they were yesterday or will be tomorrow. It's a night-long contagion of winning deceit. It's an all-expenses-paid trip into another body, for one night only, like in science experiments. The air was frosty, moderately dotted by streetlights too dim to encompass any scene in full. Flashlight beams pierced webs of lonely, darkened, tree-covered walkways to allow for shadowy clumps of children to scamper on without falling over onto the sidewalk – or disappearing altogether.

This was the one night I'd sit and wait for every year, it seemed. Probably the only day of the year I could or would look forward to, regardless of not having shit to do when it actually came. When it was so cold that you'd feel like hypothermia coming on, but that you couldn't dress appropriately for it, because zombies don't wear overcoats and mittens. Cavemen with cheap plastic clubs from the toy market, doctors with moderately detailed plastic stethoscopes, girls with long green noses and capes, boys turned half-goat, with their chests painted deep red, swinging long red plastic rapiers while evilly nursing snakelike red tails that pointed in spades at the end. Too cold to breathe but too exciting to shiver. It's sacrificing yourself to be something immortal. The one night I waited all year for.

Except for this one night *this* year, that is. Sadly, this time around, tonight, it just wasn't the same. I couldn't pinpoint exactly what felt different about it, or even if there was any exact culprit for what turned on me this year, besides the whole being older thing. But whatever it was had been nagging at me all month. Probably – maybe – for a lot longer than that.

It was infuriating that it didn't seem to matter that I wouldn't have to be the same person tonight.

I could be the real me or this shitty scarecrow and it just wouldn't make a difference, would it? I pulled a potato sack over my face, but it didn't matter that I wouldn't break character even if I were hit by a car. The whole thing seemed hackneyed tonight.

Somewhere in the trees, angry little skeletons were probably waiting for me to come close enough to fire whipped cream filled balloons at my head. And I hoped I'd find them and that things would be okay. Something rotten gnawed at my stomach, squirming in my belly.

But I tried to put it past me. I was still – and would be until I dreamt that I wasn't – a newly inducted number into the infection of the all-encompassing reality of chance. I was looking for something surprising, sure, and I really wanted to know what it felt like, but I knew that nothing could or would surprise me tonight. I walked the busy, painted streets pushing that out of my head as well as I could manage. The gnawing feeling stayed put, though, fastened, clinging, dark and red pools of blood spreading out beneath a jumper on the corner of the sidewalk, but I'm a strong kid, so for all anyone else should be concerned—it wasn't there. Anything could happen, so just let it, and forget about it.

A band of werewolves sprinted past me like a disorganized jogging team, trailing brightly colored pillowcases behind them in the wind – some of them blank white, but a few were patterned with roses, and one of them was solid green. They howled like the cinema taught them to. It wasn't far-fetched and it was extraordinary.

Scarecrows don't normally howl, but I did.

I was hoping it would feel good, but really it just hurt my cold, chapped throat. Nobody was around to hear it, anyway. Nobody that I could detect. But then again, I was a good way into being so drunk that I could barely stand. Funny that it didn't parasite my functions.

In eerie contrast, I didn't skip a beat or lose a single brick of footing as I swept up a large, bulbous pumpkin head from some dark porch and stuffed it into an empty black pillow case I'd been toting around in my baggy back pocket. I twisted the fabric until the weighty lump at the bottom was like a tetherball at the end of a cord of rope.

The pumpkin in the pillow case grew steadily heavier as I hauled it from house to house, across dark front yards and around the block, shifting the weight between frost-bitten hands. I cut through a few backyards, too and hopped a broken wooden fence that almost collapsed and took me with it. There were two skeletons on the other side. One of them had a needle pressed into the crook of his elbow. They both looked up at me, frozen, their green glow-in-the-dark skull faces haunting the crooked little yard with pre-packaged malevolence. I heard the needle snap and one of them exclaimed in pain, after which both of them ran – albeit in a slow-motion sense, as though they were trapped under water. One of them collapsed in the street just ahead. I could see his pale, dirty bare feet glowing ominously in the dull streetlamp yellow. The remaining skeleton panicked at the collapse of its companion and abandoned the frozen body, retreating into the shadows where it belonged.

Essentially, this whole night was about desertion, in its way. Hundreds of kids tonight had left their tired shells at home to let other, more meaningful things wander the streets. Pale-faced, bundled-up wooden parents sweated to keep up with them, begrudgingly leaving their ideals at home for the sake of their own pride, not wanting to be That Family who won't let their children trick-or-treat. Maybe they just didn't want to feel like their lives didn't exist anymore in the face of a night that just ended with candy, nothing more meaningful than that. Candy rules, candy ideals. And if bubble gum or caramel can overcome life choices, letting people leave one another behind for good in the canvassing of just one more block, what does anything else matter? Maybe I finally understood their reasoning. How shaky everything is when you don't understand yourself and no one has the time to do it for you. And I smiled, because you just couldn't do much about it in the long run. It would all be forgotten tomorrow.

I lifted the pumpkin over my shoulder, held the end of the pillowcase tight with both hands. Climbing up onto a dark porch, as silent as the moon.

Dangling the pumpkin a little bit as I got closer, tightening my grip at the coiled end of the pillowcase, I raised my hands again, holding the pillow case over my shoulder, tensing up the closer I got to the two people sitting there in the darkness, holding each other.

Swinging with what I perceived to be the hardest I'd ever exerted myself, I knocked this kid Lawrence against the brick wall of the house. The accompanying bushes and trees, with all their rustling dead leaves, were so loud it was a stadium audience roaring. I should have pointed to where Lawrence's head would land before I swung, because it was such a harsh yet poignantly reverential thing that I could probably have been raised up on the shoulders of the ghouls out on the street and put upon an altar to give lectures. It was a hard swing. The mushy thump of the pumpkin smashing against Lawrence's head was only surpassed in its severity by the echo of his skull splitting through a window shutter.

What it did was pull his lips away from Heather.

Her mouth was still poised in mid-kiss, though, puckered for Lawrence's mouth. Like an altered photograph.

She looked disgusting like that and hardly the Heather I'd always found so pretty. Wasn't it her that made me want to swing at Lawrence, in the first place? Or maybe I was just feeling a bit low when I got here. But when pretty people like this hang from rafters, their swinging bodies look every bit as ugly as she did, now. It's just the sour part of promise.

Everybody has an ugly side. That's why they bury people underground instead of keeping them in the public eye. That's why caskets aren't made of glass and the bodies not left above the ground. People would just piss on them if their husbands and wives and girlfriends and lovers looked like this, after so much time spent adoring them. It's an insult to be shown that ugly side. You can end up pondering just how much you really liked that person, when it all boils down to percentages.

The movies they play on cable television in October aren't the same ones they play all year round; they're the ones where inanimate objects talk, glowing green clouds appear under the cracks of doors, hands knocking on the other side – the *outside* – of a third story window shatter everyone's concentration . . . and certain dead things won't stay dead until the movie's finally over. It's a decisive action upon the senses. It brings you to something.

Merely caught in its titan ebb and flow, I didn't have a say in the actual decision-making process tonight, but I certainly felt I was a part of a resolution. Where there's demand there's supply. And goddamned whatever was wrong with the television in the living room.

Some kid dressed as a cowboy dashed across the street a little too fast, tripping over his plastic lasso. His legs at once became tangled and he fell headlong into a rusty old convertible set up on blocks at the mouth of a drive port. His face left a deep wet red streak down the side of the car as the stilled cowboy slid motionlessly to the ground. Lots of people who saw this happen cried out in shock; there were a few kids standing around under the streetlamp, dressed as skeletons, laughing at the cowboy, but I think even though their noise was all full of chuckles, behind their masks they were probably wincing too. An Indian standing by the mailbox ran off, patting the palm of his hand against his mouth as he hollered away into the darkness. Two princesses – one draped in pink and the other in white – kneeled down beside the cowboy with their long dresses trailing along the concrete sidewalk, and they cried over him.

It looked kind of staged, but it was pretty – even though it wasn't staged, anyway. It only took a second for the fallen cowboy to be surrounded by the dutifully concerned and then, through the throng, I could no longer see him. A few more seconds passed before the boy's father arrived to break the throng, to haul him up over his shoulders and run back across the street, disappearing in the darkness. Either that or some guy just grabbed an unconscious kid and made a break for it.

But I doubt that's the case.

It's a pretty safe neighborhood, here.

Back home, with the straw hat and potato sack tossed forlornly over the kitchen table, I stuck my pocket knife into a jar of peanut butter and pulled out enough to spread onto a slice of plain white bread. There was only one slice left, so I looked around in the pantry and refrigerator for something to make this seem like more of a sandwich. All I could come up with was some lettuce. So I covered the thick layer of peanut butter with a few leaves of lettuce, cold and crisp, folded it up into a half, and I leaned against the counter, looking disinterestedly at the photographs and notes pasted on the front of the refrigerator, eating my dinner.

One of them was a yellowing photograph showing me when I was really small, wearing brown pants and a green shirt that looked too tight; my mother and father and my sister Hanna were all standing around me. Yellowish silver braces gleamed from Hanna's mouth. Looming behind us – commanding a good portion of the vertical, four by six frame – was a space shuttle.

I have no recollection of whatever family trip that was, but I've never asked about it, either. It's just some phantom moment in time that's long over and the details are not really important, if ever they were. But I gazed at it, staring at myself, watching my eyes, wondering if the boy in the picture would move.

By the time I finished the peanut butter sandwich, I think it was three-quarters past midnight. Everyone in the house was asleep, I think. Either that or just gone. It was a Saturday night, after all. Nobody had school to wake up for or a job to go to when the sun came up. During nights like these, it usually would mean a silent, empty house. Creaking stairs would guide me up to my bedroom, cold dry shower curtains formed malignant shadows when caught in the hallway light, a leaking faucet crooning the echo of drips from one side of the hall to the other. Cold bed sheets wrapped me up like a baby. And always somewhere in the house, despite how chilly it was outside, a ceiling fan would be spinning, humming and squeaking and disturbing the settled dust.

The front of my dirty overalls was spotted with Lawrence's blood. When I'd purchased these things at a thrift store last week, they weren't even half as sullied as they are now. Worn and faded, but still too moderately respectable, I had to wear them jogging through the woods for a few days, diving into bushes and rolling on the ground. I'd dragged them through a patch of thorns and stomped them into a puddle. Finally I even ran over them with the car in the front yard.

And now they look like they've been hanging on a real scarecrow for twenty something years.

PLEASE DON'T LEAVE ME

a
medical
student

Peter sat outside on the front porch while Paige thrashed around inside, screaming her lungs out. Mrs. Gabriel was still inside the house, too, somewhere close to the front, slamming doors and not saying much that Peter could make out over her daughter's screaming. An ambulance – its siren wailing, itself but not quite loud enough to mask Paige's high-pitched screams – eased to an extraordinarily comfortable stop at the curve of the long, bricked drive up to the house, blocking anyone's view of the fountain.

Five or so paramedics spilled out and marched up to the front door, not looking in Peter's direction at all. They pulled the screen door open as if shoving aside somebody standing in the way, continuing the rush inside, unannounced. Paige's screaming grew progressively shrill, the clamor joined by the din of a heavy struggle as it carried throughout the front windows and echoed all throughout the gardens. Mixing with hollow birdsong. When the paramedics reappeared on the front porch, Paige was strapped down to a stretcher while a man with long black hair tied in a bun stuck a needle in her neck. The hair over Paige's face was pasted to her forehead with sweat, eyes roaming frenetically without blinking. Her chest heaved, legs and arms pale as ice, sweating, shaking against the restraints without much success. The guy with the bun in his hair asked for another needle from one of the other paramedics – a lady with a scowl on her face too strictly enforced to seem unplanned. The other two looked a bit shaken but kept their concentration substantially – their own professional frowns not as good a show as the lady's – as they secured Paige even further with an endless array of thick leather straps, tightening buckles, shooting hand signals to each other that were acted upon. Emptying the contents of the needle into a spot just below the other reddened mark in Paige's neck, they stood up and carried the stretcher toward the wide open doors of the ambulance. By the time they shoved her in, she had become weary and calm, wetness streaking her face and pooling at the eyes, and the vehicle sped off with its siren wailing, again.

Mrs. Gabriel stumbled outside, half dressed in a wrinkled skirt and white bra, her hair a mess, pulling her way down the railing of the steps and across the cobblestone carport to the fountain as the ambulance disappeared around a collection of thick, tall trees. She tossed a glass of wine into the muddled green water and screamed at the towering stone angel who stood on tiptoe with water spouting from its eyes. 'I've done all that I can do!'

Her voice was joined by more birds, sullenly chirping.

But the cherub – looking on over the house with its hands clutched lovingly to its heart – did not respond to her.

She looked at Peter on her way in, swaggering as she did so, strutting like some delirious stripper on stage, drunk and flustered and frighteningly heartbroken. 'I'm sorry, Peter.'

Then 'You should marry into this family and take her, along with a new name, someplace far away. To the other side of the sea. So I can get that fucking girl out of the Gabriel family directory.'

FOUR MONTHS EARLIER:

He arrived in town with nothing more than a suitcase of clothes, a letter of admission from the university – with disordered dates and times haphazardly scrawled on the back that he sorted out on the bus – and some classes to get to, post-haste. Thoroughly ill-prepared for this, he pushed his suitcase breezily into his new life, a step ahead of him. After a day of pushing the suitcase down the halls ahead of him, slightly weary but not enough yet to sigh, sitting at a window seat watching some cop walk two little boys across the street, Peter met a lady who said to him 'Hi. I'm Helena Gabriel.'

She was a forty-five-year-old widowed woman befriending a twenty-two-year-old transfer student at the medical university and nothing seemed out of place about that.

Tightly pulled into a ponytail at the back, her sleek and controlled haircut accented a smooth, forgiving – if not babyish – jawline, giving her the look of a woman a lot younger than she actually was, despite the wrinkles at the sides of her eyes and the dark, bruise-like bags under them. But her smile was warm and so was the voice she let drift around the confines of the coffee shop, like notes from the radio next to the napkin dispenser on the countertop. Not out of place, she looked like any number of the rich ladies Peter had seen walking around the distinguished main street area, as if their husbands were all at work earning the profound bundles of money being spent right before his eyes. And being that she looked a little short of patient in this particular little café – comfortable yet not-quite comfortable with it – Peter wondered if perhaps they were all just the disaffected bored wives of medical professionals from the college, lost in the world their husbands built and treated with social formaldehyde. He wondered if there was a veneer all around him, in every step taken past him.

He looked at Helena Gabriel and saw a friendliness easily attainable.

Peter looked into the future a little and pictured what he might possibly look like after a life of medicine. Tired and old, but comfortable and still healthy? Like everybody else? All he could really see, for some reason, was a handle-bar mustache and a grim collection of blank expressions in his arsenal of professionalism. He smiled at such playful pessimism.

He wasn't really the sort of person to look too distantly into the future, so as far as he was really concerned, the only future he had in anything was as a student, during this semester. And maybe the next semester, as well. Simple and straight. At the moment, a student and nothing more. Save thoughts for the future for when it arrives. Hopefully he'd be a surgeon when the time came, like his grandfathers before him. Masked and sanitized, commanding the glint of a scalpel with effortless precision.

Mrs. Gabriel sat down next to him on a whim, shortly before the place closed, having been taken by the way Peter looked at his watch so nervously, running his fingers through a sheaf of curly brown hair, every so often reaching down under the table to blindly assure himself that the suitcase was still there. Helena recognized his behavior as that of a harmless boy with no surety as to what would ever come next. And it was cute. She liked that. It was nice not worrying about what might happen, especially when there was always so much to worry about right now, right here, every moment of the day, every day. She envied his suddenness.

She'd guessed him right, as it happens, for when she sat down in front of him with a cup of straight black coffee and said 'You're new. You haven't been here before. And you don't have a clue how you're going to spend the night,' Peter responded, after a time, with Do I look that pathetic?' And he'd smiled so sheepishly then, a bit embarrassed, going through one of those things that people just go through. But then he'd gotten over it and that was that.

Helena laughed sweetly and told Peter that he looked just a sight more than lost. What had really been running through her mind, though, was charming, handsome, smart, and possibly easy to get along with.

And that's precisely what was needed.

Peter bowed his head genially. 'My ability to make preparations of any sort whatsoever is absolutely appalling, Mrs. Gabriel. I haven't a place to stay, tonight. And that is my dilemma.' The predicament of his situation was not at all pessimistic but light-hearted and a bit incredulous. Very much straight to the point. And Helena liked the way he talked, all of carefulness, the delightful sincerity, and above all the pleasantness.

Pleased to have made the young man's acquaintance, she asked him to call her by her first name and then inquired if he intended to find a job in town. 'Of course,' he said, because otherwise he might not be able to find a stable place to stay, which was what would be called for in aid of his studies. He was sure there would be a decent place to crash somewhere, once he met somebody on the campus, but that acquiring a place entirely his own after the first semester would be more ideal progress. Helena laughed and said 'Nonsense.'

But Peter insisted that living on his own was actually better for his studies. To which she laughed.

'No. I meant nonsense, you're not going to crash on somebody's cold tile floor. You're not a pile of cans. There are other ways to go about handling yourself while saving up a little bit of money. And a stable environment is surely more attainable than you think.'

She lived in a ten-bedroom mansion, not too far from the university, with her daughter Paige, who was twenty-four years of age. Her husband – Helena offered without Peter having to ask – was dead. There was plenty of room, if Peter didn't mind staying in a poor old widow's near empty house set at the back of two lonely acres of private property, studiously gated and guarded by a high, wrought-iron fence. It could have been taken as a most foreboding prospect, and that's how she told it – in a jovial attempt at being modestly ominous – but all in all, that was where she stood and the offer was on the table – so to speak – if Peter chose to take it.

Just as she suspected he might be, Peter was left both thankful and bashfully appreciative, assuring her that – although almost broke – he would provide at least money enough for rent, just as soon as he could find himself a job in town, maybe as a waiter or a gas station clerk. Helena nodded, said that would be fine. He put his suitcase in the back of her large black car and together they drove to what was, essentially, his first-ever home away from home, a hidden manse in the woods, under the cover of looming trees, bordering a wide gray lake lapping at the shore with sluggish, salivating waves.

When they arrived outside the house, swinging the car around the drive port, it was even bigger than Peter had first envisioned upon Helena's already overwhelming mention of ten full-sized bedrooms. But of course, the only house he'd ever lived in held but four. The mansion was very far from the main road, with a massive stone fountain at the conclusion of the driveway in front of the house, at the center of which stood a baby angel poised on one foot, arms crossed and wings high, with twin rivulets of water spurting up from the passages of its eyes.

He was given a room down the hall from Helena's daughter Paige, whom it was assumed was fast asleep – as per usual during the day, Mrs. Gabriel noted. But when Peter threw his suitcase onto the bed in the room designated as his, a sudden movement in the curtains kicked his heart down into his belly and he almost choked.

'Who are you?' asked a girl who stepped out from behind the curtains.

'I'm . . . *Peter*,' he said, startled and sounding as if he might just be unsure about that.

She sighed. 'Hardly,' she whispered to herself. 'You're just another.'

'Pardon me?'

The girl moved away from the window. She stood fairly tall, deathly pale, with short-cropped black hair and bright green eyes that didn't search much as she looked Peter over. She gave him a glancing once-over, but then turned her attention back to the blank wall next to him. Peter found her rather beautiful, even if she did give off the appearance she'd been living inside of a closet for the past ten years. 'I take it that you're Paige.'

'Yes,' she said without reluctance. 'And you're another.'

'Another what, exactly?'

To this she laughed. 'My mother met you and has taken you in, I presume?' Peter nodded. 'Then you're just another boy from the college who needs a place to stay for a term, and who is willing to fuck any random forty-year-old woman to succeed at making those goals of being Big Doctor turn into a stunning reality. Congratulations.'

Peter almost choked again, but he didn't have to ask what the hell Paige was talking about because the clues were suspiciously there all along and he'd half-suspected it anyway without all of that. Mrs. Gabriel – no, *Helena* – had been very forward and sweet to him right from the start; commenting on his handsome features while raising her eyebrows, touching his hand whenever she'd laughed. Of course, in his head Peter had just mildly entertained it as an overblown exaggeration of some creepy fantasy all boys fear when a friend might have asked another friend if they'd do it with a ninety-year-old woman for a million dollars? And yet, *Helena* was no ninety-year-old fossil, but still, the situation had been close enough to have such things *entertained*. How long would that go on in life if the answer was Yes, just one time?

Would-You-If? seemed, suddenly, no longer a game, like the one he was kind of caught in now without even trying – the one that everyone, after a moment of serious thought, would reply to with 'Hell yes.'

But this? She wasn't ninety, of course, but…

Peter was a bright kid. In some matter of years he'd likely be a doctor. And he certainly didn't need to become a whore to get there. Repeatedly he told himself she was not ninety years of age, was not fossilized, was not on life support. Was not freshly back from the grave. Contrary to this, the woman was very pretty, resembling a naturally aged version of Paige. Upon further thinking, Peter supposed a woman like Helena would not have to make such a deliberately desperate search for suitors anyway, because her suitors should, in all actuality, be the ones dropping to her feet. So the pleasantly awkward picture that Paige was trying to paint could well be rolled up and tossed into the wastepaper basket for all Peter cared to indulge it.

'I know what you're thinking, whoever you are,' Paige said with no little amount of distaste.

'My name is Peter, I said.'

'And I don't blame you. My mother isn't too old. And she still looks in her twenties, anyway. Perhaps a bit like me, even? And hell, maybe you didn't even know what she was up to, in the first place. In which case I do feel for your lack of intuition. But before you say another word, just remember that my mother likes the boys bearing special gifts. If you're good with your tongue, welcome home. You can expect to be treated dearly.'

With that, she pushed forcefully past him and made her way toward the door.

'Wait,' he spat, fumbling more than stating.

Paige turned, swinging her hair rather dramatically, sounding like she only pretended to be interested in what he could possibly have to add. 'Yes?'

'This isn't what I want. I was just sitting in a bagel shop. And Helena…' There he stopped himself, catching a possible slight error he felt he might not want to make, feeling suddenly that he was already eerily close to the girl's mother. 'Mrs. Gabriel walked up to me. And it was obvious I needed a place to stay. That's all. I had no clue. I haven't done anything wrong.'

Paige smirked. 'You're a pretty young boy. The thoughts were in there somewhere, I'm sure. Weren't they?'

Peter's face grew red. 'Well. Yeah. I suppose. But . . . Jesus. How the hell could anyone really guess that?' He held his hand out to the girl, as if she would possibly offer and answer on his behalf. Then, beginning to feel a little used in more than one aspect of this situation but trying to push that creeping notion out of his head, in strict defense of himself as well as the generous Mrs. Gabriel, he added 'She hasn't made any passes at me. At all.'

'There's still time yet, kiddo.' Paige tapped at the front of her closed lips, smirking. Her face was void of humor. 'Remember what I said about the tongue.'

Sleep came with great difficulty that night.

Like he was pre-disposed to carry off the unease well into the furthest reaches of subconscious, he dreamt inextricably of having sex with an old lady in her coffin.

Knotted tufts of gray hair fell from the lip of the casket and fluttered to the floor as he gently pushed into her, so delicately, taking care with the brittle bones to avoid the corpse snapping into pieces, until at last the woman's body was left with nothing on her head but a crumbling scalp.

When he woke, the pillow was damp with a nauseous sweat and he felt like throwing up.

Over the course of the month, Helena not only prepared meals every morning and night for both Peter and her silent daughter, but also lent him the keys to a small black car in the garage so he wouldn't have to take a cab to the nearest bus stop or purchase a bicycle. He was given one key each to the mansion's front and back doors – or one of the back doors – one for the boathouse in the back she assured him he'd probably never use, and even a key for the private guest house on the island in the lake – which she also assured him he'd probably never use – as well as for two other vehicles in the five-car garage, one of them being a motorcycle Helena described as 'The pissed-away livelihood of the late Mr. Gabriel.'

With so many keys on his ring, Peter felt like a damned caretaker. But it was nice and it relieved him of feeling like a stranger in the awkwardly large, empty house.

Helena would take him out drinking after classes, whereupon they would become accurately smashed every night, most especially the nights in which Peter professed an express need to study. Soon they were quite popular amongst the deep swimmers at the lonely, clandestine, out-of-the-way pubs she'd take him to, far enough away from the bustle of the more college-bound bars full of talk of term papers and acts of budding, one-night romance.

It certainly wasn't the campus life he'd envisioned having at such an exemplary university, but not a bad one either and he toasted to that – and often. It seemed that before long, he could just barely remember what the inside of a classroom looked like, viewing his study-times as hours without study in the bounds of smoke-burnt barroom walls. But the more she pushed him, the harder he found it to come up with passable ways to say No. And so the nights swam by.

He'd try winning himself over by asking the bathroom mirror 'When a young man of twenty-three – he'd almost absent-mindedly passed a birthday, wading through it with cheerlessness in silence and privacy – is offered endless alcohol and new shirts every day, where does it state anyone has the ability to deny that sort of stuff? Or the right to it?'

But always after this, at the back of his mind where all the forlorn wallflowers of bad tidings hung about, came the uninvited picture of himself pinned between Mrs. Gabriel's legs, hearing her grunt 'Harder' as she pushed his face into her. It sent roughly hewn chills down his spine. It was crazy – they'd never had a single moment where it seemed she had any interest in him outside of escaping sobriety – but all he could do was haunt himself with the antagonizing prospect of being a male prostitute. With each new gift – a new shirt, a fitting tie, a smart, shiny watch – Peter grew steadily more wary of his charming yet somewhat odd hostess, waiting for the oncoming solicitation. But as for what he and Paige had discussed the first day in, so far there came not a single incident leading to the actions he so feared. For all intents and purposes, when it really came down to a description of Helena, Peter could only truthfully account 'She's lonely and she needs a friend.'

And that was all he was left with at the end of such searching. No explanations, but a lot of guilt trailing no body and a weariness that weighed more than twice himself.

Whether it was the cold alcohol constantly swimming in his brain, the awful few moments of rotten study adhered to at any moment it was possible to escape Helena's need to have company, or just the plain strangeness of the dark old house that nobody else ever entered save for the cleaning lady – Ida – Peter began to suffer dreams of a very disconcerting nature at night. The dreams started out relatively harmless, with Peter waking up in a cold sweat, not able to recall what he'd dreamt.

These were nagging dreams, but no matter how hard he searched for an association, they were simply not related to the drinking, to being a bad student, or to the debacle with Mrs. Gabriel. And then, as the dreams became more vivid, involving ice and darkness and staircases and fields of wheat and storms and whispering and people stamping their feet, Peter began waking up from these mounting slumbers sprawled across the floor in the attic.

The first time this happened, he'd no clue whatsoever of where he was and he started screaming so loud it woke both Paige and Helena. The latter wore a dark frown over her face, tipped a glass of clear liquid into her mouth and only mumbled a coarse '*Great*,' then returned to her own room. As for Paige, the poor girl had tears in her eyes. And after her mother stormed off without a word, she did the same herself, slamming the door behind her, leaving Peter to himself, dressed in nothing but boxer shorts, shivering, alone in the frosty attic.

Soon, it turned to him waking up sprawled out over the staircase that led from the foyer up to the second floor rooms.

As the dreams worsened, his trips out with Helena grew rapidly less frequent. She'd share a drink with him in the kitchen late at night, if they happened to be there at the same time without intending to, more and more neglecting even the mention of going out.

This worked out somewhat fine for Peter's studying, or so he deliberated at first, and he'd feel better in class not entirely hung over, but it didn't sit as well with him, as he felt it should have. For one, it actually felt kind of lonely now, with no constant drinking partner, hardly any conversation with Paige and a dwindling security of his frail future in school as a student of whatever sort he'd become. More than that, he also felt a little abandoned.

Gradually, Peter started to feel as drab as the house looked, sapped of energy by bad dreams and an incriminating distaste for looking at his study books.

Sipping from a small glass of scotch one morning, out under some dead eucalyptus trees, pondering how the waves lapped at a thin, corroding wooden dock that led to the boathouse – which was itself a heap of sinking wood that could probably stand to be condemned – Paige came out to join him. She wore no shoes or sandals – as always – and her feet were unwashed, stamped in dirt.

'Tell me, Paige. Why is the house so beautiful inside, but yet everything else around it in complete disrepair?' he asked her, motioning toward the abandoned landscaping and then to the clearly unsafe dock.

Paige was ever paler out in the open, dressed in a white skirt that dangled just above her darkly bruised knees, with little flowers sewn in at the hem, under a green and yellow flower-print shirt, with straps hanging lifelessly over her shoulders that didn't do much to hide her sunken chest and alarmingly evident bones. Her clothes were much wrinkled, which for some reason made her look even skinnier, packing more and more of her away into nothingness. She probably didn't eat so much. Drinking from a carton of milk, she spat a mouthful of it out onto some rotting oranges bundled in a heap by an ant pile, watching the ants wash away. 'Nobody gives a shit about anything around here. And I'm surprised you don't know yet why the house alone is kept so neatly, or why nobody goes through the rooms but the goddamned maid.'

Peter turned to her, the dark bags under his eyes themselves looking like bruises, fitting in with the rest of these sorrowful people. 'What does that mean?'

'Well,' Paige said, sounding tired. 'You're getting a lot more from your stay here than I thought you would. You know that you are, too.' The corners of her mouth curled up a little, but she caught herself, and just that short second of emotion in her eyes was all that he got. 'Not in the *naughty* way, however, *if you know what I mean.*' Peter's face grew irritably red, both with prolonged embarrassment and sudden impatience. 'Anyhow,' she continued. 'Ida says you haven't bagged my mom yet, which is kind of funny, but I think that's only because mother thinks you have what I have now.'

But Peter didn't think there was much to play so coy about. The gloom shadowing his face turned to an even darker shade of worry. 'What is it that you have, Paige? What the hell are you even talking about, if you'll allow me to ask?'

Paige just smirked again, the way she had the first time the two had met. This was all getting too out of hand.

Without turning back toward the house, she threw her open hand back toward it and lazily gestured toward the floor they both held rooms on – a streaming set of windows on the second floor. 'I have *them,*' she said. And then she walked away.

Peter looked up at the empty windows of the second floor.

In each of them, simultaneously, the peeled corners of curtains all fluttered closed just a tiny bit – as though somebody had just snapped the curtain shut, somebody staring out at each window from each room, from the same corner of each leftside curtain – and then they were still again.

Peter jumped back. Suddenly, it felt so cold outside that he convinced himself that the chill pulling his spine around in his body was a matter of weather and not anything to do with that he now felt as spooked as a little child lost in the woods during twilight. And he darted toward the house, after Paige.

More often than not, the three tenants in the house kept to themselves, with Peter left feeling as if everything he was used to was more awkward than it should be.

He was drinking more than he ever had in his life, alone in his room, wading through textbooks like murky water, his hand scribbling nonsenses that he referred to as notes, inevitably unable to read his own script in class.

At school, he was losing track of his studies to the point where he didn't even know what classes he took. He showed up late to most of these classes, going through the motions, working on his papers while lectures droned on, wondering how the hell he was even still enrolled, scrawling with pens long run out of ink, forgetting everything only moments after supposedly learning it – or at least halfway hearing it. And then he'd drive back home and slip into bed and swirl around in nightmares that bled into waking with profound mysteriousness, agitation, and a growing horror.

Helena was slumped in her chair at the table in the kitchen when Peter came in and tossed three of his textbooks onto the counter. She asked him a question just as the textbooks hit the countertop, drowning out her words.

After a few moments of silence, a few scattered sighs, she asked again. 'Want a drink, Peter?' Helena's features were wasted and used, as though she hadn't slept in weeks. There was no sprightliness in her appearance, where before there had been life; the Helena he met so long ago at the cafe was now reduced to what was really hiding behind that veneer of money and desired youth, a veritable corpse that still walked. Now that he'd had time to truly study her, she really didn't look so much like Paige, at all and looked older than she actually was, too. The gloom in her eyes spoke nothing of the desire for fun anymore; more of the weariness of a life that simply did not change, but rather tended to nurture monotony as the days grew on, feeding it stale, unneeded ribbons of flesh from her side. Maybe she was just a bad dream and it had always been this way.

For the first time, Peter felt trapped in a castle whose king was never actually seen and whose subjects were not permitted to leave their allotted placemarks on the courtroom floor.

He suddenly felt like making a break for it.

'No thank you, Mrs. Gabriel. I think I should study.' The words felt stupid and fake. He was lying. To himself or her, it was unclear.

She looked dismayed, sighing. 'Hmm. Peter, you haven't called me that in quite some time.' More time passed. Then 'How is school going?'

But Peter didn't want to talk about school. Factually, he didn't know anything about that subject, anyway.

'What's Paige's deal?'

Without another word, Helena got up and walked out of the kitchen, disappearing into a tight stairwell reserved for the help this mansion was not currently employing, up the stairs and into her room.

When the sun left and the windows turned black and it was cold outside, as winds rattled the shutters, he knocked at Paige's door. The sound of the quiet repetitions were too loud in the stillness of the hall. Brooding echoes drifted from around the corner, sounding much like bad recordings of knocks on doors, a telling reminder of how awfully out of place it sometimes was to make a sound in the house, of how displaced everything else in his life seemed under this roof. From inside, after knocking too many times, Paige's distant, disconnected voice told him the door was open. Inside the room, she was sitting in the corner, holding her knees up to her chest, shivering under the open window.

'I've been having really bad dreams, Paige.'

'About my mother?' she quipped dryly, trying to be humorous but failing at it. Her face was pale and she was sweating profusely, though the room was nearly glacial.

'Would you drop that, please? I haven't touched your mother.'

Paige giggled a little and for just a fraction of a moment she seemed to have more life in her than there had ever appeared to be, before. She turned red with unease. 'I know, I know.' Her legs came down and she set her feet into the thick carpet, scrunching it with her toes. She turned back, looking toward the window, watching the lake for probably nothing. When she started speaking again, it was with a fragile composure he'd never heard from her before, which was, quite surprisingly, almost reasonable friendliness. 'By the way, I was only kidding that first day you came here,' she said, putting her forehead to the glass. 'My mother never brings people home. She called me that day before she brought you here and asked if it would be alright if her *friend's son* came over to stay in the room next to mine. I think she was just trying to do me a favor, or herself one, actually, by setting me up with a boy. Or at least somebody reasonably within my age bracket. She gets worried that I'm such a fucking recluse. It's the only time in her life she's shown that much interest or worry, I think, and so she's relatively new to the whole process. Someone ought to tell her that bringing a stranger home to play with her daughter isn't what most other moms would do.'

Lightening up, for the first time actually enjoying Paige's company, he leaned against the doorframe with his hands buried in his pockets. A breath of fresh air was exactly what was needed, and Peter basked in it, easing up. He laughed a little to himself, training his eyes at Paige whenever she seemed to have glanced away and wouldn't notice. She just barely blinked, sitting still as the wall. In quick motions so as not to intrude, Peter shifted his eyes about the room, noticing that the only things she had hanging up on the walls were a mirror over the hope chest and a straw-stuffed doll wearing a straw hat over her bed. The doll had buttons for eyes; one black and a bit smaller than its colleague, which was brown.

'So I was just playing with you,' she added, turning about to face him. 'About my mother. She's not a whore who fucks local students for a hobby. Not that I'm aware of, anyway. She's a bit lonely, yes. But aren't we all, these days?' She tapped at the window, flicking the glass with a fingernail. 'I wouldn't exactly put it past her to try getting laid by a younger kid like yourself, but so far as I know, she never has male callers.'

Exasperated, melting into the doorframe, Peter sucked in and let out a deep breath, rubbing his hands together. 'Jesus, Paige. I've been regarding her like a swindler for two months now, because of you.'

To his surprise, her smile seemed even more sincere than her sneering. 'I know. I can keep the joke running pretty good.'

'I've noticed.'

'Have they talked to you yet?'

'Who?' Peter asked, getting confused again.

'Keep an ear out.'

'What?' he asked, feeling like she was having him for a laugh, again.

She looked up toward the ceiling. 'Keep an ear out, Peter. That's all.'

The odd thing was – and this he hadn't even admitted to himself, yet – that he'd been doing exactly that. For weeks now, he'd been hearing scratching sounds coming from the other side of the ceiling. Sometimes footsteps, sometimes whispers, but upon investigating upper rooms and the attic, nobody was ever there. When sober for some reason or other at night, he could just make out the sound of Paige mumbling in her room. At first, he figured she was speaking to somebody on the telephone, but when this turned to going on for all hours of the night, at random points during the day as well – and he was pretty sure she had no friends whatsoever – he'd sometimes pick up the receiver elsewhere in the house to pretend to make a call, always met with the dial tone. He'd asked Helena how many lines the house had. 'One,' she'd grimly sighed, and then asked 'Why?' but not really seeming to care for an answer. As soon as Peter would mention Paige talking at night, Helena either sparked up a different conversation or, as was her failsafe route, she'd just up and leave the room.

But he did not let things die there, even asking Ida about it. The sometimes maid, always a quiet, studious cleaning lady, said to him in a very quiet tone that he should just ask Paige and not her, and then would say no more.

The footsteps in the attic at night turned to violent stamping, just as in his previous dreams. Peter would jump out of bed and race toward the landing, pull the attic staircase down and climb up, all in less than a minute. But nobody was ever up there, of course. In the attic, it was always icy, even when the weather outside was balmy or warm and the rest of the house was regularly air-conditioned.

The reality of dread in his dreams grew worse.

In them, he'd be carrying a profoundly heavy block of ice down the staircase, afraid to drop it for some reason he could never exactly pinpoint. Scared out of his mind for dropping the block of ice, he'd wake up in a cold sweat on the staircase, panting, his hands cold and shaking.

Paige started locking her door. Sometimes he could hear shuffling sounds from under his bed, until at last he fled the second floor altogether and started sleeping down in the central den beside a brightly lit fire, on the warm bearskin rug. Every night the fire would go out – of its own accord – while he slept. Sometimes it went out even as he fed it.

Sleeping instead in the kitchen, with the stove turned on high to warm the room, he propped himself up in the high-backed chairs with pillows and a thick blanket.

He'd wake up with bruised legs and migraine headaches, sometimes in the midst of tumbling down the staircase, absolutely drenched with sweat, his skin icy and stiff. Or face down on the bearskin rug. He'd sit up for as long as possible, studying walls, staring at an open book with medical terms that read like a foreign language, blindly shuffling through magazines without seeing the pages – all of it looking like foreign languages too, even the pictures.

Trying to get Paige to talk to him – which she'd long stopped doing – he looked at himself in the mirror and didn't see himself anymore. It was a parody. Some stick figure. Some jerk. Some scared jerk.

Her voice carried through the door one evening, whimpering, half-whispered 'I don't talk to *anybody* in this house.'

But Peter hadn't knocked or said a thing. He was only just standing there, unbeknownst to her, half crazy and predominantly scared. She could not have known of his presence outside the door, so clearly she was talking to somebody else in there. There was so much shuffling going on inside the room that the door was bumped, even though where Paige's voice emanated from should have been the opposite end of the room, by the window. A dry brushing sound against the other side of the door made Peter take his ear away from it quickly. He knocked twice and everything went absolutely still. No answer came from within and eventually he went back downstairs into the den.

A faint but unpleasant smell drifted to him that night as he tried with no success to find some semblance of decent sleep, shamefully curling up to the walls and lingering in the room all night. In the shadows the fire cast upon the walls, there seemed to be bugs crawling along the wallpaper. The awful smell in the room would be gone by the time he woke again. And it was the same upsetting smell that sometimes came from the attic at night, when nobody else was around. Musty, like decay and mildew or the bones of rats, trapped behind a dresser. Things progressed like this until Peter was delirious. In the dark, he'd pop a flashlight on and the shadows would dance in ways they shouldn't. He thought about leaving medical school.

Then came Paige's nightly screaming. And then came the ambulance that took her away.

to carry handfuls
of rain

'It's only more of the same old shit,' I mutter to myself, with a distressing premonition of agony crawling around inside me that isn't comfortable at all. Tempting, hiding away behind my heart and the sick stomach filled with baseless desires that are themselves just old, faraway dreams that never quite amounted to anything. In the dark, I make my way through the silent kitchen and pull a chair from the table. The overall silence of the house is impressive, as is the architecture, and in a way it makes me think what a labyrinth a good deal of years can be, as I have woven my way through countless halls just like this and nothing has ever seemed to arrive at something that could resemble much of a conclusion, no matter how much I coat the situation with whiskey drinks or sugar. Weakened by what I start to think might be the last threads of determination splitting at the ends and coming apart, it's difficult for me to process that this burglary was worked out in carefully cut seconds and minutes, yet I've thrown a lot of those so carefully timed tables right down the gutter by weaving about the glass tables and gilded high-backed chairs of the dining room, aimlessly, and watching the stars twinkle outside through crushed-velvet curtains that I had to drag aside with what felt like a boatload of effort on my part. The possibility of being arrested tonight seems like a fair bet.

PLEASE DON'T LEAVE ME

But I'm just so tired. Dressed all in black so as to fit in with shadows in dark rooms, my presence should not be realized, clicking my tiny flashlight on and off in the house and thus effectively defeating the purpose of such precautions, playing the beam across the kitchen ceiling like that's an okay thing to do right now, I can't help but think that joy is more addictive than anything else. It vanishes so fast, you know? I don't even *like* diamonds. In fact, this whole burglary thing is a bad idea tonight, because I've consumed a good deal more gin than usual. And I'm just so . . . *tired.*

My brilliant plans turn out to mean nothing and casually, almost with a very determined laziness, I creep through the rooms, running my fingers lightly over the exposed teeth of pianos, stopping to admire family portraits dating back to senior centuries, until the small suede bag attached to my belt is filled with jewelry and crystal ashtrays. I've even found a small porcelain figure of two children, a boy and a girl, pushing a wheelbarrow, and their eyes are, confoundedly, small diamonds.

Pausing at the threshold of an anteroom opening up into the largest private library I have ever seen inside a residential home, I consider, actually, going back upstairs and slinking underneath the coverlet of one of the guest beds to have a nap. But at this moment, I hear a pair of feet softly shuffling in the room above me, though since this place is so massive I wonder if I'm only just hearing things. But I also take notice of water running up in the room, shutting off, feet rustling carpets and beams, and then silence again. So it snaps me out of my malaise, but doesn't cure it, and slowly, back to the task at hand – if only in a confused, nearly emotionally empty way – I enter the library.

The tomes and volumes rising over me are tidal in scale, packed into towering oak shelves, braced with tall ladders on running tracks, and I can feel the bones in my body crushing beneath the weight if this were to become an avalanche. The room is so quiet and the carpet is so thick, I make no sound crossing the room. I feel like a man on the moon, except for that all around me are oil portraits stretched onto wide canvasses, severed and stuffed animal heads with gleaming black eyes forever watching nothing, and dotting every other cleft of wall space not otherwise occupied by the massive shelves of books there are countless rifles under which are pinned small golden plaques bearing the namesake of each firearm.

Most of the books on the shelves are huddled into shadows. I can't make out any of the titles because my head is spinning.

After what feels like the rest of the night, I exit the manse through a back hall that needles its way from the library out to a garden of chrysanthemums, carrying the bag of jewelry and a few rifles I pulled from the walls.

On Sunday morning, after having pawned the rifles for a handgun, I stand over the Audrey Heights Bridge, emptying round after round down into the oily black water. I imagine myself climbing up onto the rails and diving down into the cold river, gracefully, like an angel swooping down from Heaven. But what I really do is pull myself over the side with great effort, so that by the time both my legs are finally, mercifully over the side, I am out of breath, out of energy, and I haven't whatever it takes to rally any of it back, however much or however little that it would require to be able to turn this around or take it back. And pitifully, the dive turns instead into an inelegant, lifeless plummet down into the water.

The river hits so hard I don't have time to take a breath before my body is defeated and the churning waves are overlapping me. In my mind, I'm picturing somebody else doing this and how they might bob up and down at the surface of the water for a minute or so, splashing, their body going against the head's will, trying to save itself. But my body isn't doing that. I'm down below the murky surface, without sunlight, my head expanding with the pressure. It hurts a lot more than I think it should. Involuntarily I gasp, and sucking in liters of filthy, fishy muck, my eyes pop open and the water is stinging until I think I'm too numb for this kind of pain and – instantly, then – forget that it hurts.

Choking on the water, no more oxygen to keep this hurting anymore, I finally start to thrash around, a late-comer in the grand tradition of what probably appears to be self-preservation. It's futile, in retrospect, but only if I start to fool myself into thinking this flailing is some sort of attempt.

Gradually, my arms are still, legs lifting as the torso falls faster. Wonderfully, all pain gone, all sense of environment disappears, I think I am falling from a plane, a powerful wind pushing me up with a hundred hands. Maybe my eyes close, but it's too dark to tell and I'm too numb to figure it out.

Diamonds spin about me in magical, twinkling columns, dancing and carving revolutions around crystal ashtrays. A small porcelain boy and a small porcelain girl, their eyes twinkling too, they push a fragile ceramic barrow about my head, circling my head in a moving halo. Rifles are raised, saluting, popping in unison. I fall through the air, not feeling a thing, because my nerves are dead.

Everything else in me follows suit. When I brush the bottom of the river, dragged by a slight current, I don't know that this is happening.

PLEASE DON'T LEAVE ME

the
lobby
rats

You start to wonder if there are ever moments in your life when you could have stopped and declared 'This is a turning point.' But what you take for granted is usually the thing that's keeping you, well . . . alive. So small moments when I actually pay attention to things, they only bleed through like it's an accident.

The Donastle's engine comes slowly down the rail, whispering its way along in provocation to every corner of the night. Meanwhile, the engineer is sounding the bell so much more loudly now it seems for the sake of any pedestrian within a county or two's pass, or even those since passed on, below the ground. Loud enough to shake the line between life and death. This is the first running of the train since it reduced a teenage boy and his more adolescent sister to photographic evidence, half a year ago. There are searchlights on the face of the train now, massive white bulbs stripping the night in a sinister, almost embarrassing scope. The trees outside my window look naked as my desk rattles and the lamp shakes. Some jellybeans in a dish rattle and clink against themselves in the porcelain. The pen on my page of notes skitters over the course of a few lines, the ball-point circumspectly narrating key points in the discussion that I have planned for Harrison tonight – namely a new development for us, namely an elephant. The train clicks along the tracks and it fits well, making the night and everything within it fit well. I would expect owls out there to be cheering. This is the way it's always supposed to have been, this steadily moving railway ghost, skipping tracks with a curious beat resembling so very closely the blight of a complete black-out; the always charging, unimaginably suspicious Donastle slinks, clawing at the wooden beams of the tracks. The black train whose engineer waves at shadows as the machine pushes forward.

I've seen him do it before. He waves at dark stands of trees, at murky abandoned lots, at seemingly nothing.

That haunting wave perplexed me once to the point where I joked about it with Harrison just to avoid really talking about it, should it be considered out loud. That the look in a train conductor's eyes could haunt me like that was the first time in my life that I realized how fragile everyone is. I've watched that man wave into a bleary night, robotic but smooth, convinced. Me, the shadow. Me and Harrison in the dark, gazing on in troubled awe at some nameless railway engineer composing music of bells and unimaginable noise, making contact with complete blackness. Harrison and I now as unimaginable as the train's awkward, rolling plight. Us: some amount of nothing, some shadows. Some difficult bruises in the dark.

And he's back there, the Donastle's conductor, in his saddle, his throne, sounding the bell. The Donastle Line can't ever die so fast as those kids did when they stepped over the tracks that momentous night. That bell's proof, isn't it? This bulk of smoking, screeching steel will be here even after *I'm* dead. After everybody who puzzles over its irregular night prowling along the lines that cut Hampstead Haw like some cumbersome bag of bad drugs itching to earn as much as possible for what little it's actually worth.

But what worth it does possess, this place, it's being upped, slowly and steadily, by me and my friend Harrison. To us, at least. In a way.

And I stop writing, turn the lamp down and gaze out the window at the train on its re-birth run. I'm having a hard time coming to a suitable conclusion as to whether this is progress or merely the way things go, so I am unsure if the good feeling I'm getting watching the train pass isn't just nerves. It's possible that something as truly unsettling as the train is only serving to overshadow the sick feeling in my stomach I've had the past few days, thus pulling an illusion that stuff agitating me isn't really that important. Or maybe this black cloud over my black cloud is just in my head. After all, it's just a train. And Hampstead Haw is just a town. Me, I'm just one person.

Harrison and I make two. Maybe that's all that's needed to get things going.

Harrison knocks twice on the door in surreptitious sets of three and this is the way he enters, smoothly so that I do not feel tempted to pull the revolver from a drawer and panic and forget that everything's not as dire in the world as it seems sometimes.

His head's clean shaved. The formulating scar of a recent motorway accident shines on his operated head. When he comes in, appearing before me humbled and yet somehow guiltless, it's with a wide smile that swallows the room, ingenious and perfect. It's full of a bittersweet love and boyish honesty, this smile. This is what makes Harrison the single person I feel comfortable with. But his smile starts to disappear a little when he comes closer and by the time he's reached my desk he's nondescript, which is something that can only be done when he tries really hard not to show any feeling. His mannerisms as he takes the seat in front of my desk appear cut up and forced, sequences pasted together to form a prescribed action, working hard against that smile as it manipulates what's in him and what's not. He's nervous and it's apparent, but still the fellow smiles. This is Harrison all the time, actually.

When he finally stops this agitation, resting in the seat opposite me, he rubs his shiny skull. I can practically make out what Harrison probably looks like without skin. It's not a comforting thought, not really fair for *him*, and quickly I dash it from my mind, replaced with the fading tick-tick tick-tick of the train outside.

'I feel naked, my friend,' he says, red-faced. Still rubbing at the bare skin of his head, avoiding the surgical incisions, he looks at me quizzically, scanning me on the status. His embarrassment's endearing and instantly I feel better about what the source of his agitation must be, hoping it's not the same one I have, that disgusting sense of doom in my roiling belly. 'I need a hat.'

'You look like a skeleton,' I say jokingly, smiling.

'Some bones?'

'Some bones. How's your head, Harrison?'

Finally, the smile resurfaces and a cool breeze spirits through my bellyful of diseased and antsy butterflies. A trickle of relief works its way down my spine. Part of the only reason I think I'm still alive is that smile of his. Though I am hesitant to suggest Harrison might not actually exist – that he's merely some guardian angel no one else can see – I still feel obliged to thank him, silently, privately, to myself, for being here. It gave me a reason to finally trust somebody, that smile of his. He's still unable to keep from touching his smooth scalp every few seconds. The monotony of this squirming fills me with a mollified lungful of air. I sigh it out, thinking I hear rain at the back of my head, but putting that aside in favor of choosing not to notice that I can still hear the train passing.

Harrison was hit by a train himself – though not the mournless Donastle, thankfully – just last month while trying to pass over the tracks in a crowded thoroughfare on a bicycle, racing through lines of stopped cars as they sounded their horns in alarm and protest. Their warnings went unheeded and the train clipped the back-end of his bike tire as he shot across the tracks, sending him off into the sky like a rocket. His shiftless body collided with the unyielding base of a fire hydrant, instantly splitting his head open. He has little recollection of this happening – a faint remembrance of soaring through the air – but onlookers described it in detail to the papers and he was a minor hit in town for a week, which is funny to think about, considering what we make out of our free time around this place. So there he was, spending the week hot, miserable in hospital, at the Grand Lady of Peace, not eating; his body locked nearly immobile in a bed in a room, not entirely unlike prison and scary enough to spook the daylight from him. He was understandably unhappy there and it's nice to see him out. But while being nursed back to health, I'd visited him twice, once bearing flowers as a sort of joke, but the next time loaded with skin magazines, the likes of which got him ejected from proper nurse care on account of crude suggestive talk falling from his eager lips in their presence, while thumbing through the magazines. From thereon the care of my friend was conducted only under the provision of male nurses, which I guess is what finally got him to force his body well again. So in a roundabout way, dirty magazines in this case helped bring a man from his lowest low to the sunny prospects of health and happiness.

If you can call the way he winces when he moves his head Sunny.

'Feel's like I'm fucking naked,' he says, looking down into his lap while rummaging through his coat. He pulls out a large plastic-wrapped bag of almonds. 'Got a bowl for this?' he asks, grinning, pulling the plastic off the slightly torn bag. Dust from crushed almonds spills out.

'Where'd that come from?'

Still grinning 'That shit down on the street. I put a fist into his guts and he caved in easy. I didn't even take the old bastard's money, just the almonds. All the almonds he had in the cart. This shit's gonna last me until I puke it out.'

Disappointed but not surprised, I ask 'Why'd you give that old man trouble, Harrison? He's harmless. And pretty old, man.'

He scratches his bald head. 'Don't know,' he says, gazing out the window.

And this is the setting of our evening.

Wiping ink from the side of my hand, I mark off a few notations on a yellow notepad and confer with Harrison. We calculate distance and match it with the evening's transit runs. Later, we're to put bullets into the head of a household's pet elephant, owned by the man and wife Faresea, but left mostly in the predominant care of a little girl named Melissa, their daughter. I was standing in line at a supermarket when I overheard the little girl gloaming on about the elephant, which was when the concept entered my head and I wheeled around to see the speaker, the protagonist. This is how I found Harrison and I's next line of work. Fair-haired, wide-eyed, with a sharp nose and full pouting lips that must earn her the sympathy of all who behold her, Melissa's the perfect little child, apparently. The tiny gradeschool proprietor of this baby elephant that Harrison and I are going to shoot to death in her backyard much later tonight. In the middle of a typical, regular, spread-out suburban crop of well-off plots of land in a northern corner of the town, the Faresea family has caged a wild baby elephant in the bounds of a half-acre of lush property; safely hidden away inside a surrounding fence of thick, round oak posts. It's eerie. It's beautiful. And soon it will be over.

Harrison spills a handful of almonds into his lap, sighing. Picking them up and placing them back into the bowl, eyeing me, he apologizes. But I don't really care about the spilled almonds. He looks a little nervous and I just want him not to be. 'So we're going to kill some kid's elephant?' he asks, staring glumly at crumbs of almonds in his hand as if they were the dust of his own bones, wiping them away slowly.

'Yes. Her elephant.'

'Geoffrey, what the hell kind of kid has a pet elephant?'

'I know. It's amazing.'

'We're killing an *elephant*?'

'An elephant.'

With better care this time, Harrison pulls a few of the almonds from the bowl and takes one into his mouth, barely chewing. I've always rather liked almonds myself, but I'm not sure why since I could never really taste them all that well. It was more the texture that intrigued me about the almonds, and the delightful snap when bitten into. Watching Harrison, I felt a distinct sense of separation from him, and it did not sit well with me; I'm not so sure that Harrison had much of a particular fancy for the almonds either, and even though I tried to shake it off, I felt a little disturbed at how they were procured. This wasn't really how we were used to *making a difference.* It seemed like an omen. In my head I could hear that old man crying to himself. Most likely bleeding. *Still* bleeding.

Then the sudden silence in the room became effortlessly uncomfortable, switching my mood in an instant. My mind raced ahead of me, left me. We should get back on track here.

Still looking out the window, although it's difficult for either of us to see past the glare from the lamp, Harrison reaches into his jacket pocket and pulls his hand out clutching a small collection of bullet casings, tossing them into the small wastepaper basket by the desk. Then he pours what's left of the bowl back into the plastic covered bag, seals it tight and ties it closed with a simple knot. Handing it to me, he asks if I might store them in the desk before he eats the whole bag and gets sick, which I am happy to oblige as I've actually seen the boy eat until doing just that. He thumbs through a book on my desk without really looking at it. Then after a time, settles again and, sitting up straight, his smile is back. 'Alright,' he says decisively, with a little restlessness welling in him that I can see but choose not to comment on. 'If this is what you want, then let's go kill that elephant.'

'It's kind of a baby elephant, by the way. It's a younger model. I guess they call it a calf. It's a child, but quite a good deal bigger than the girl. Bigger than the both of us put together, actually.'

'Who is the girl?'

'It doesn't really matter. We're not shooting her. I don't really know much about her other than that she seems to be the only one out there who pays much attention to the elephant. Checking out the place, it doesn't appear she has any other friends, either. That's sad. Or maybe it's just how things are. But of course I wasn't looking into that much, so maybe she has friends at school. Really, I'm actually a bit in the dark about how a father will let his little kid outside all the time with a fucking elephant. I would imagine it could be dangerous, surely. Right?'

'Of course. Maybe her parents aren't much fit for parenting,, Harrison says. A good observation, I might add.

'Whatever the case, they shouldn't be a problem, either. They turn in kind of early.'

'Age'll do that to a person.'

'Scary.'

At a quarter past midnight, Harrison rolls up in a taxi one block over, jumping out. He's a thin, wicker shadow sprinting across the dark pavement and disappearing into an alley before the car can fully stop. When the engine suddenly cuts and the brakes screech and the vehicle skids, the driver hops out, bumblingly, attempting some kind of half-assed pursuit, but gives up a few yards from his cab, shaking his fist at the darkness. He is left shouting ineffective strings of angry curse words, with nobody around to care. Sighing so loudly I can hear it from where I'm sitting, the driver gets back into the car and slowly begins to crawl off, undoubtedly still eyeing the shadows. A couple minutes later, Harrison comes up from behind and he hops the bench, sitting down, breathing hard. 'Forget that guy,' he says. 'Cab drivers need to figure out how to avoid getting ripped off before this kind of thing is really *my* fault.'

It bothers me slightly that we have very important things to do and Harrison's been fucking around like this all damned night. Honestly, what he said struck me as funny. Especially coming from him. The way he says something like that could make even the *cab driver* see some humor in it. But we're not playing jokes, him and I. At least not tonight. I need him focused. Or at least I need some kind of semblance of it. Harrison is like a typewriter to me and if it's written on his face, I know he feels it inside, to a proportionate degree, so I need at least some show of focus behind this silly crap with almonds and the cab driver. In all fairness, however, he's dead right about cab drivers.

Excuses aside, this is building a better future for us in Hampstead Haw. For the two of us, this is a small stop on the way to raising a small town's worth. We're headed somewhere, here. And nothing will stop that.

On a bus that will take us closer to where the big houses are, a chill crawls up through my legs, climbing me to the top, to the back of my neck. It is pinching my temples tightly, urging me to wince. I feel like shivering, but this passes, thankfully. It slowly becomes rather surreal when homes occupied by single families begin taking on the appearance of small mountains. One wonders then how a bullet would hit anything significant, like somebody shooting a single bullet into a canyon from the lip of a cliff. You get the feeling that extreme measures are needed.

Harrison checks his revolver while I check mine. He stares at his ghostly reflection on the inside of the window in the bus while I look past it, to the graveyard, the headmarkers of which dart by in the swimming black night that surrounds the lit monuments like the bus is skipping lakes on a stone. The first headstone I can make out without ambiguity is a serious, looming giant guarded over by a foundationally disturbed angel, tottering headless over the eulogy. This is the deformed gravemarker of Hampstead Haw himself, the luminary's etched stone gathering pricelessly average mold and grime. Seen from even the most disarming and attractively deceptive angle, it still looks like a slum, this cemetery. The simple indifference of nature has transformed reverence into rot over the bones of the man who so long ago founded this town out in what was, at that glorious and hopelessly-irrelevant time, the middle of fucking nowhere. As ultimately useless as any pick me-up really could be, seeing that headless angel still soothes some growing disquiet in my cold bones, every time I see it. It brings back old times, because a few winters ago, in fact, I was the one who pounded the stone head off that angel. I did it while passing through the graveyard on my birthday. And to this day, it's never been replaced. In a way, it's definitely made me feel a lot more useless and invisible than just existing on a regular plane ever could, but adversely, in this way, the reality that the town's very founder is so off-handedly and assuredly neglected has been a helping hand in understanding that if I have any purpose in life, it's time to find a way to serve it before I'm dead myself. And by now, the chipped stone at the neck is smooth and worn. The man's obviously no longer so important, whereupon once he was, I guess, some kind of giant? Enough to have been buried in so lordly a fashion by his successors. Not that it lasted. That was then and this is obviously now. The graveyard is spreading, slowly and surely, thanks to Harrison and I. The rest of time does not give a shit about this place or for the man who was Hampstead Haw. And soon it will forget all about everything to do with either.

When we arrive outside the Faresea estate, we're pushing our way past the barbs of a rose bush in the little girl's neighbor's yard, stepping through a small, skittering brook, approaching a low part of the fence before it turns into the wooden posts that are too tall to climb. Harrison's got a hat over his head. He doesn't usually wear hats and the steadfast irritation he's feeling about his appearance is starting to worry me. He's just not focused. We are supposed to be focused and I've already been having a hard time with whatever's been slightly upsetting my nerves, so it doesn't make me feel any better knowing he's feeling out of sorts, too. We're worth nothing, him and I, if we can't give ourselves purpose.

These huge yards, how foreign they are to us and how small we become in this paid-for, well-kept wilderness. It only adds upon the doubts in me that we belong here right now, in our plan. And naturally, the very notion that we don't belong in our own decision-making process is numbingly sick. This squirming feeling gets so tense that I'm clutching my stomach here and there, feeling a second's breath from a hospital-bed-worthy sickness. Something is worming around inside my belly that's what I think an uncomfortable situation feels like, but it's a confusing feeling and I'm not sure how to take it. When we get to the fence, I can see the elephant.

'I thought you said this elephant was a baby, Geoffrey. It's supposed to be a miniature, you said.'

It was supposed to be a miniature, because when I saw it just a few days ago it *was*.

But we stand there, Harrison and I, in miniature ourselves now, in awe, staring. It's fucking huge, the thing. Actually, it's the furthest thing from a baby elephant that I can actualize in my head right now. This elephant's so old and towering it's practically ready to keel over and give up the massive ghost before we can make it halfway to shooting it in the head. This is a large, *old* elephant.

I am legitimately confused now, because I saw this creature just days ago, last. And it was only a child, then. It was practically a baby. But things don't get old this fast.

'Maybe they've switched elephants.'

True, but why? 'Picky elephant fans?'

'Who the fuck knows,' he whispers, appalled. '*Look* at that thing.' Thankfully, his voice has lost the hesitation and suspicion and this makes me feel a lot better. He's confounded, but in a way that's like being sickened. And in such a state, this is going to be easy to eliminate the elephant. Actually, I'm climbing on his words as I might climb mountains if there were any at the ready outside of these huge mansions. It feels like I've just woken up. I try to smile at Harrison, now, but I can't. Nonetheless, I feel indomitable. So I make the first move and we are suddenly crunching the grass on the greener, Faresea side of the fence, where I am trying to consciously forget the terror in my weakening bones since on the outside, in my stride, I probably look pretty confident. Trying to draw on that fly-on-the-wall image of myself walking, alongside the steady and determined pace of Harrison, it's the climb of a roller coaster again, but I don't mind the climb as long as it's a good stretch of time before the next fall. I want to be ready for the fall and I want it to be exhilarating. I want it to be this vast beast falling dead to the grass. Feeling at once more grateful for Harrison's bottomless trust and friendship than ever before, I try to think only of that and not the centuries-old Baby elephant we get closer and closer and closer to. All too soon again, experiencing the roller coaster, rushing toward the earth too fast for the moment.

Slow down, I say to myself, to the scene before us. Please?

There is nothing to stop us entering the full, openly-lit center of the yard and we coast across the lawn matter-of-factly, stiff grass underneath us crunching loudly in the night. We approach the elephant where it stands, near the back porch, gazing on silently into a small, dense stand of walnut trees, and already it looks smaller to us, younger and fitter. The physical change in the creature's size is instantly haunting. Up close, it looks like it could charge over us and stamp our bodies flat as pavement, it's so fit and agile. It ruffles an overgrown set of ears at us, curling the trunk lazily. Inspections race through every glance the harder the stare I give, but there is no mistaking it, up close the elephant looks *smaller*. Younger. Almost more so than upon my initial – albeit fleeting – casing of the grounds, a few days ago. It does not make sense.

I look over at Harrison and he has tensed up all over again, in and out of this now, his fingers twiddling with themselves. The panic in his eyes is something I'm hoping I see only because I'm starting to panic too, but he looks at me the same way I am looking at him, and that sick feeling in my stomach is threatening to shift into a full bodily virus. I can feel my arms shaking, muscles contracting. That whole confidence thing is at best a script I'm now playing through. What a horrid performer I must be, too. I hate to have Harrison see me like this, but from the looks he's giving me, I think he's too horrified to notice.

The mistake of it being a baby could have been a mere oversight on my part, for all he knows, so the dread in his eyes is just that much more foreboding.

The elephant cranes its head toward us to look me in the eye. Buried in the threatening gray of its skin, those terrible eyes are glossy, wide, and black. From the bright and encompassing light showered down from a few towering lamps on the back porch, I can see my own reflection in the elephant's eyes, clear as a mirror. Suddenly, I don't feel so sure about even standing here. I might pinch myself or something.

My concentration is severely lacking and I start to stare at the elephant. Me and Harrison, I'm seeing us reflected in the thing's eye. But in this reflection, we look like children again – the way we were when we were *children*. That silly uncomfortable wave of brown curls dancing on my head is there in the picture, along with Harrison's neat and timely flat-top – the one his mother always insisted upon. Two little know-nothing losers we were back then and it actually makes me smile for a split second. He looks like a sailor and I look like an orphan. Two useless little lobby rats, gnawing at life expectancy. In the elephant's eyes.

Harrison's timid voice 'It's smaller than when we got here, Geoffrey.'

I know. 'I know . . . I know.'

'Did you notice it was bigger before we came this close? It was bigger and older.'

'I know, Harrison...'

'It's a baby, now. I blinked and it's a baby, now.'

'It's still bigger than we are,' I say, which doesn't mean anything at this point.

'What the hell is this?' Harrison is wiping his eyes. His motions are so dreamy I feel he may not be able to work his own gun. I grasp his elbow and tell him to hold still.

'Let's just try to put this into perspective, Harrison.'

'Right,' he says, not answering me in the saying. Just saying that. And then again 'What the hell is this?'

Before I can put my hand around the revolver in my holster, my tense fingers instinctively clutch at my stomach instead, followed so closely by the other hand that I don't know why, but balance is lost. I stagger and both hands shout for equilibrium, pushed out and awkward. Harrison jumps back, falsely alarmed. I wave my hands to signal it's okay, though what it may be I'm trying to say is *okay* is of course vague and appropriately debatable. My body feels like it's turning backward to a time when sickness was easy and natural. But though I wish I could vomit this one out, I can't. There's no bed and nobody to tuck me in and feed me a spoonful of medicine. It's just not that kind of sickness. Whatever is crashing through me is *not* natural. *This* – as it were – is not natural. Harrison looks sick, too. He's repeating the last question over to himself, murmuring. Until his pitch suddenly gets higher and he asks 'Are we going to kill it?'

That's the plan. Yes.

I pull my coat open and grasp the handle of the pistol strapped in its holster, but it takes me a few gulps to flip the strap and pull it out. We aim our revolvers at its head while it stares at me, eerily ignoring Harrison. What are we waiting for?

What are we waiting for?

I pull the hammer on the gun. A deep metallic click echoes into the night and across the light-swept lawn, disappearing into the shadows and playing in the heavy undergrowth and thick, bewildering trees. I'm ready to shoot, but I somehow don't know what to do about it. Harrison's gun does the same and in my stomach I feel each reverberation. My hand starts to tremble, which I don't want Harrison to notice. I feel less than who I am and embarrassed to be whatever that is in front of Harrison when this was my idea.

I don't know why, but I even feel embarrassed in front of the elephant.

To avoid having my trembling trigger hand commented upon, I steady the gun with both, gripping as hard as I can manage, pushing the barrel against the elephant's head as it stares at me, unresponsive. From its throat comes a reserved rumble, then it blinks its eyes and just stares at me. In the big black pupil, I see my reflection aiming the gun at my own chest, directly at my heart. The way the reflection carries, it looks as if I'm facing off with myself, some sickening feeling I want to shake so badly I suddenly feel the need to lay down, I get so dizzy. Momentarily, I feel anger toward the elephant for doing this to me, then a thicker anger at myself for entertaining the absurdity that this creature's the root of my problem.

What are we waiting for? We just have to shoot the elephant in the head and leave. And then we'll both probably fall asleep at the office and then wake up and then split up to do whatever it is we each have on our personal agendas tomorrow. And *tomorrow* I don't *have* to do anything; I can take this queasy feeling back with me and tomorrow I can lay down all day if I still have to. If I have to throw up into the sink I can do that too, all day until my throat is eaten away. *Tomorrow* I can do anything. Anything that I want.

The thought bounces fiercely around in my head. *Past tonight I can do anything.* We just have to get there, safely. So what are we waiting for?

What the hell is it we're fucking waiting for?

'You'll put yourselves to death with worry, moreover,' the elephant says, looking at me still.

Harrison cries out, backing six feet away from the elephant in what looks to me like two gigantic steps. Frozen in my place, I just stare. We still have our guns raised, but Harrison is even further from the elephant now, having been scared practically out of his shoes, and I feel at least a thousand miles, at that.

The elephant blinks, slowly. When the lids are once again hidden and it becomes just those two black eyes, mirrors showing me to me, I have to turn away. But you can't aim a gun and turn away. Gradually, I am able to force myself to look it in the eye, again. Harrison edges closer.

'What the fuck was that?' utters Harrison, softly, not himself. Not in charge of himself or in charge of anything. I'm worried about his gun, which is waving around, at the elephant and the trees, at the ground, at me. Pinwheeling.

'Are you sure you might not better enjoy just lying down and going to sleep?' the elephant asks me.

...decisions become increasingly erratic, as I have lost the faculty to know anymore the difference between saving myself and preserving what I think I'm supposed to be...

And I know that the biggest difference between feeling okay about the rain and merely feeling like it's Okay For Now is nothing that a sincere and more probably effortlessly delivered fall from a disastrous walk along a bridge cannot pretty much nail down in a single sentence with '*I refuse to go to the funeral unless it's open casket.*' But I think I am losing sight of what's standing ahead of me. I focus on the elephant. It brings me back to the moment and I suddenly recalled why I was propelled from it so. Then bullets cried out.

Harrison screamed again and shot once. The bullet entered the elephant's head and it groaned, reeling back. I pulled my own gun back and involuntarily shot upward, over the elephant, over its head and into the darkness. The stray bullet sunk tunelessly into an ugly black crowd of skulking trees, disappearing. My stomach felt like a schoolyard playground where a fight was just breaking out, all motion and no thought.

Still standing, the elephant blinked at me, slowly. 'You make a lot of mistakes,' it reflected. I couldn't help thinking that maybe such an assertion was dead correct.

Harrison stared at me. 'This fucking elephant's talking to us.'

'I'm talking to myself,' it returned. 'And it feels like a pitiable endeavor.'

Harrison waved his gun in the elephant's face and yelled for it to keep its mouth closed. I winced as he shot again into its flank.

The elephant took a single step back to balance itself when Harrison pulled the trigger again and another bullet slammed into the elephant's skull, burying itself in its huge head with the sound of a large boulder hitting the ground. The blast shoved the creature backward, but it righted itself before it was toppled. With the fatally bleeding elephant faltering a bit but otherwise still standing, with its eyes all the while on me, with gunshots ringing in my ears, Harrison screamed and shot it again. Staggering, the elephant looked momentarily toward my friend, but swung back yet again to stare at me. I aimed my gun at its eye but could not pull the trigger.

It groaned and then, too calmly, muttered 'The things you do not understand about yourself far outweigh the constant noise in your head about other things. Just look at this. Look at how you're acting.'

Harrison fucking fired again and I shouted at him to please stop, thoroughly livid that he could not better compose himself. He protested, but I grabbed his arm, again pleading with him to stop even while I myself still had my own gun raised at the elephant's gushing head. The towering beast blinked even slower now, pursing its wrinkled, leathery lips, kissing the cold night air. Then it moaned. *It is huge again, the elephant. Massive and ancient. My gun is aimed upward now at its head instead of directly ahead of me. It's so tall I couldn't see a reflection in its eyes if I had a fucking step ladder. I can't understand what's going on.*

'If I die, then you do, too. Eventually, anyway.'

Harrison pulled away from me, nearly falling over in the process, and aimed at the elephant's head. And it looked like he might just start firing until the gun was empty. I made a move to grab him again, but the elephant's ceaseless chatter held me transfixed and trembling.

'You can shoot all you want, Harrison,' the elephant said wearily. 'I'll be dead soon, regardless. And you're killing your best friend. Is nothing sacred to you? You and your modest plans? You have so much to do, don't you? Like to kill your own best friend. The only person in this world who actually *likes* you, who respects, admires, and even *loves* you. You'll just kill him off, shoot him in the head. To serve some purpose, some plight that itself is not really even founded. You are as unimpressive as forgetfulness.'

Harrison fired twice more, pulling me from my inertia, and I rushed at him, shoving him away from the elephant, hard, screaming as much as pleading now for him to please stop. To *please* hold off until we could gather some kind of hold on this. The elephant continued to stagger, shaking the ground beneath us. It lost its balance and I had to dive backward to avoid its path, landing with my face in the grass but picking myself up fast, confoundedly ashamed of myself and brushing the dirt and dew from my jacket. Christ, what the hell was happening?

Planting my feet firmly in the grass, I swung the gun up to pull myself back upright.

'What the fuck are you *talking* about!' I screamed, and with the sound of my voice splintering the firing of a bullet also sounded, and it crashed into the elephant's side; I'd unintentionally fired my gun only because of the crumbling system of nerves guiding my body now; I hadn't meant to shoot at all. In fact, the crack of this second misfired shot alarmed and surprised me and I fell backward, into Harrison, who pushed me away dutifully. It seemed nothing short of puppet strings would keep me on my own goddamned feet.

Finally, I found what I needed to gather some kind of hold, and I wasn't shaking anymore. This was our night. We were not at the mercy of some household fucking pet. This was *our* night. 'Enough!' I yelled at Harrison, aiming my gun slow and steady at the elephant, whose face was now dark, shiny and wet, the eyes mostly blinded by its own blood.

The elephant wailed into the darkness of the yard, howling. It was nearly dead now.

I pulled Harrison back and smacked his gun away. His eyes were wide and pulsing, his face flushed. He looked unkempt, taken away from himself and lost. He grabbed my jacket and pulled his lips to my ear. 'What's happening?'

...I do not know what's happening...

When the elephant regains its balance, I am questioning it sadly with my eyes, sort of stunned, sort of dazed. But I'm not so scared anymore. I'm able to hold the gun with just one hand. All that races through my mind is the prospect of an end to this. A very near end to this night.

The elephant sighs, unstable, near death. A haunted glare is cast down from its drenched eyes, fixed on me. It feels like insects are crawling the whole of my body. I don't want to be here. I don't want to be me. I want the night to get even darker and to eat all of us into a deep, long sleep.

Then, a voice from behind – rickety as stairs but feigning an incredulous authority. It booms out like a pre-recorded joke, like thumping a radio as it blares deafening static down a flight of stairs into pitch black. The echo it trails seems contrived as a studio funnel. 'Alright, there! You all hold still and don't move!' Some far away bravado that doesn't matter this close up.

I look behind me and I'm surprised to see the little girl's father *in his bathrobe*, barefoot, pointing a shotgun directly at me. 'Put your guns down,' he says, trembling, scared. 'The police are on the way, so just don't cause any trouble or so help me God I'll kill the both of you.'

Harrison's eyes are wild. He's no longer in control of himself and he raises the revolver at the man. I lurch to stop him, but the father screams at me, his voice cracked and petrified. Backing away from us, he shrieks '*I said don't move!*'

For a moment, we are all still. I can hear the elephant behind me, staggering in the frosty grass, the ice melting as blood from its body splashes all over the ground. I imagine it falling on top of me, crushing me. It could take me out of this situation right now if just such a thing were to happen, with its own death adding mine along with it, just keeling over right on top of me. Harrison and the frightened father look like two cowboys who have just buried the perfect shot back and forth to each other at the exact same time, both haunted with the realization that, though they each are victors, both will die perfectly self-same deaths, too soon to change the course of events.

But behind the old man with fractured, tired eyes, his hair pale and broken in the porch light – a weak heart pumping through the bathrobe – a light pops on in a window in the second floor. In the yellow light a tiny little form appears in silhouette, slowly reaching for the curtain. Harrison is staring at the man with the shotgun while I watch, as in a dream, his daughter Melissa's silhouette floating in the window, ghostly. It only takes a second, but a few seconds is a lot longer than what it takes for a bullet to change the whole world around us. From the lamplit open window a shrill whimper . . . '*Daddy?*'

At this, Harrison raises his revolver toward the window. The father turns back, his face instantly drained of color as Harrison fires a single shot toward the window. And the silhouette is in that instant knocked back, out of sight. The man in the bathrobe shrieks and his gun is systematically turning from me to Harrison, but I shoot the girl's father in the head before he can pull the trigger. The shotgun falls to his feet before the body can lose its balance and, long dead, it keels over onto its side. I train my gun now on Harrison, though I don't know why and I wish I could stop.

'Put the gun down, Harrison!'

Every time I build my concentration back up it is once again shattered. Harrison's staring at me, his lips moving but no words coming out. Then he aims again at the elephant's head. I realize that with the shoot-out in front of me, I had almost forgotten about the elephant behind me. I swing around and my gun goes toward its head, too, and I feel like the whole cat-and-mouse concept is being taken to new, gigantically inappropriate levels.

The elephant is pale. No longer dark and menacing, its silvery skin is glowing white, thick as paste in the porch light. The elephant now looks more like a giant maggot than the mighty enigma it had been minutes ago.

As ever, Harrison and I are both aiming our revolvers at the elephant. It feels like I have been doing this since I was born.

Or as if I were just born tonight, doing this in hours that have stretched long into years. Its eyes are damp and running. Large splashes hit small pools of blood where it hasn't already dissipated into the soil. Then a shot rings out and Harrison is thrown off his feet. I turn in a matter of seconds and just barely make out the blurry semblance of what must actually be the little girl's mother – the dead man's wife – pointing the late father's gun at Harrison's corpse. My eyes focus through fresh tears and it's certainly her, alright. She's crying, shaken by the kick from her husband's gun. Bewildered, I shoot once, but I'm frantic and reasonably scared out of my mind. The bullet hits a vent in the roof's surface behind her and chimes out into the night. The mother is lost in her own world now, not taking this chance to aim her gun at me. Her eyes are sunken into pits, the thick veins pulsing so far from her neck and the sides of her head that her hair is coming undone. Before she is dragged from whatever hell is happening between her ears, I shoot her in the center of the chest and the inopportune woman falls, gasping and gurgling, sputtering, convulsing, and finally ceasing.

Behind me, the elephant is trying to speak.

It seems to take forever for me to turn and face it. I watch the landscape swivel about me on a carousel. A house looms over the bodies of man and wife. Black and red is splashed over everything. A window up at the corner of my vision is shattered and covered in thread-like spatters of it. The fence. Not too long ago, Harrison and I had climbed that fence full of surety and destination covering the grumbling weak pits in our stomachs that we could not fully admit to each other about. I watch darkness encompass me. It trails, lingering in black wisps not entirely unlike smoke. The whole backyard feels like a giant prison cell and I am turning around to face the elephant, the last occupant.

The elephant's face is black in the murky light, glistening with blood that is steadily pumping from the many holes in its skull where Harrison shot him through.

'You have no more days left, you understand,' it croaks, unable to speak much above a whisper. It narrows its eyes to scold me, effectively making me feel like a child. The whole thing makes me sick.

Defiant as one could ever be 'You won't haunt me.'

The elephant gurgles, laughing so sadly. 'Who am I to haunt anyone? You will do it to yourself.'

'This is going to stop right now,' and I raise the gun to its head. And this fucking creature is my height again, I realize. Now just slightly smaller, looking me eye to eye, and I press the gun to its wet, leathery skin, smearing blood as I stumble so close to it I'm actually leaning against its bulk. As close to the very center between its eyes that my staggering mind can process as the center, I press the hot tip of the barrel and hope it burns through to the nerves.

'That I could be you,' it forces out, making me dizzy, spitting thick globs of blood in my face. 'You don't quite know what you're up to this hour, so you'll kill me and that'll be the day.'

'You shut your mouth,' I whine, compellingly childlike. My voice doesn't sound right.

The elephant laughs. Sadly. But there is no real humor in its tone.

I'm still pressing the barrel of the revolver between its eyes, but I feel like I'm prone in a hospital bed. Weak, at the mercy of an aid. Whoever wants to help me. Whoever *has* to. Which makes me look over at the pile of limbs and bones that used to be Harrison. I wish I could will him alive or take his place. The sight of his crumbled body is really too much for me.

'You can't believe it so you make awkward decisions, now.'

'Believe *what*? What the *fuck* are you talking about?' I've had it to the neck with this fucking elephant.

'That I could be you,' the whispering death throes announce, wryly, tired, and with great effort ruffling the enormous ears on its head. 'You don't know that I'm not.'

Tired of my malfunctioning eyes, I look up at the elephant and smack its face with the gun. 'You're *not* me. You're an elephant.'

'I am *you*. I'm you, Geoffrey. Basically.'

Ingenuously, I decide to empty all the bullets from the chamber. Into the elephant's eyes. The gun is hot in my hands and after every round has been discharged I'm still pulling the trigger. The clicks are small and harmless, now. And I have to escape this. And I have to kill this elephant. And...

'*Hold it! Halt right now! Lower your weapon! You are under arrest!*'

Slowly, cinematically, retracing steps from the last time I did this here in the yard, on a carousel plays a living reel backward, seeing Harrison's sad remnants first, then the dark clumps of trees, some parents, some blackness, some holes in a second floor window, a lot of blood, all of it in all, a vast expanse of dark green lawn in the quiet night pooling around everything, a nameless emptiness in my stomach....

...some kind of purpose I can put my finger on and scream *Yeah!*

'*Put the gun down or I will shoot you dead!*'

When I can focus on the speaker, it's an officer. A patrolman. He's talking about handcuffs and consequences. I stare at him like he's made of fireflies that might just putter out and disperse.

So the father – so long ago – hadn't been putting us on. The cop – a single officer – late. This is pitiful. This is what they find, a suburban back yard full of corpses and a man with his gun pointed at a dying, convulsing elephant. I wonder to myself if the elephant itself isn't throwing the cop off his confidence. Whatever the occasion or cause of alarm, I doubt he'd come here expecting to find a bullet-ridden elephant.

'You are under arrest. Put your gun down or I will shoot you *dead.*'

What am I waiting for? What am I waiting for?

Sunlight rises vampirifically over Hampstead Haw. When that wild, wet and running bulb in the honest sky, when it crawls up above the horizon in Hampstead Haw, the vampire's head, it bleeds the land dry. Every shadow is eaten alive, drained of blood. I've spent my entire life here, wasting it day by day. But then, no longer willing to stand for it, Harrison and I started to do something about it. You can make things better if you focus more attention on them. It came about harmlessly by constructing feather-bombs in trash receptacles downtown to blow up homeless people rooting through garbage. It was like nothing we'd ever dreamed, seeing this happen in person when we expected only to read about such misfortunes in the morning paper. We exhumed coffins in Cawhale Cemetery and buried trigger-response mechanisms that exploded before a downcast crowd of heads one Saturday during a funeral. When the panic rose and the mourners scattered amidst the blasts from the graves all around them, we shot into the crowd until nobody was alive except some kids, and we spotted a puppy dog that took off yelping but died of heart failure before reaching the futile cemetery fence. I started to dream of how we could change this town; build it up into nothingness, becoming legends nobody would ever know. In dreams I romanticized our projects as things grew worse (or better) for Hampstead Haw. I dreamed that Harrison and I once shot to death a roomful of devotees looking over a comatose patient. It felt like it was real, that it could be entirely real, so next, in reality, we shot at bicyclists, injuring some of them. I dreamed we hung scores of people from the trees in Gavin Park—awake, we planned a blanket sweep of the city. We had maps of trails of reason. Little by little we watched the cemetery grow, one person at a time, until the staggering crime rate and rumored panic was our doing. We started canvassing entire neighborhoods, slashing tires on hundreds of vehicles in one night, letting the town know that it was going to be special. In small ways. Before I dreamed we surrounded the town in gasoline and burned in alive, before we lit up an abandoned house and more homeless people were lost though already long since forgotten anyway, we watched in from the seat of my ambitious dreams. From the bottom of the hill looking up at Hampstead Haw. The vampirific sun ate the flesh of the new day and we shot at what was left. We blasted our way into a new era. We made Hampstead Haw priceless. That's what we would do.

The revolver is still aimed at the elephant, which is now swinging its trunk around in dying throes. *What awful things can happen?*

My arms creak, leaden with meticulous springs. I feel mechanized and lifted with levers, all rusted machinations or elephant bones stuffed into me and electric by force. The revolver is slowly raised toward the patrolman as he continues to shout into my face. Warnings, protestations, proposals, alarms, meaningless words, period pieces, all with a beautifully stern finality. And all the sound rushing into my ears suddenly tightens, gets sucked up into a funnel and is pulled out of my head. For one agonizing and confusing moment, there is utter silence. And then, like my ears popping in the atmosphere on a jet plane, a single, solitary, and momentous thud.

It's the hollow thump of his gun, clicking but not firing.

The poor officer's face falls into itself. He's so pale and shriveled up, he looks like he's just been exhumed. The empty click of his barrel sounds off in my head and without a further moment's hesitation I spring the barrel of my revolver and wind the empty shells out onto the lawn. They fall to the grass, glistening in the porch light, hissing through cold, dark blades, out of sight. The cop is still standing there, frozen, lost in paralytic dread while I thumb in a few fresh bullets, wind the barrel loudly and snap it closed. Casually, quiet, and unassuming, I raise the gun dead ahead, putting it right in front of my field of vision so that I see the shaking, pale body of the stick-figure police officer capped off with a blurry gun as its head.

I focus my eyes on the back of the gun, then ahead toward the paralyzed body, then back at the gun again, and I shoot the man in the head. Blurred behind the gun, his body falls and the night is now left completely silent.

It stays like that forever, until from behind me a tumultuous crash erupts that shook the ground and my sense of balance and with it I fall, too.

When I turn around and the elephant's splayed out on its side, cold and dead and shriveled in its skin, I suddenly realize how fast my heart is pumping and that it actually physically hurts.

The landscape begins to spin and I may fall into the sky if I don't seek some kind of shelter, so I crawl on my stomach toward the overbearing mass of the dead elephant. My body is magnetized to the ground, biting into the dirt, so that it's difficult to raise my head, and still clutching the gun I grasp and grope at the grass, pawing at the dead giant while I flop around, completely dazed. I crawl along the dead gray body and up its side, which is smeared with blood. Pulling up onto my knees, leaning against the soft upturned belly, I turn my head to find Harrison, and each second feels like I've spiraled around six dozen times. I am completely disjointed.

The gun I rest atop the elephant when I am finally able to get on my feet again, but I have to turn around and lean back against it to stop the spinning. That's when I see Harrison and start to softly cry. Only now does my stomach finally release its stinging and I throw up down the side of the elephant, falling back to my knees in the soiled grass and pulling at clumps of it to get closer to where Harrison lays. His face is drained of color. I push his mouth closed and pull his lids down, but it's not enough. The gun comes freely from his hand, unquestioning, and I set it back in the holster, clip it tight and zip up his coat. Slowly, I walk back toward the elephant and brandishing a small knife from my sock, I saw the upturned ear from it and carry it back to Harrison's body, using it to veil his dead face.

With no deliberation left in me I stomp over the boardwalk of father, mother and cop on my way out of the yard, ferociously grinding my heels into their broken faces as I pass, snapping their silent jaws underfoot. The walk across the lawn is lonely and agonizing, but before I can realize what's happening I am nearly two miles into the night, slapping my hands against the top of the steel fence surrounding Cawhale Cemetery. Lifting myself to where some of the bars are spaced wider, I slink in between them, silent as skeletons, and climb the hill toward the moonlit grave of Hampstead Haw, the man nobody remembers.

What's left of my life is just barely visible up at the top of the small hill, standing over the plot of grass under which lies the coffin. All around me, underfoot, for an acre or so, are coffins. I walk toward the one at the top, glancing at other headstones as I pass and I can swear there are a couple side by side for me and Harrison there, but I don't stop walking to investigate the inscriptions.

The man who was Hampstead Haw says nothing as I adjoin what's left of the fresh round in the revolver to his soundless, time-eaten headstone, chipping his name away with flames eating me from the inside.

PLEASE DON'T LEAVE ME

bringing it to
your mouth, biting
into a frog

At the bottom of the staircase that creeps upward along the walls of the inside of the bell tower like the steps are hesitant of getting too close to the ledge, I'm wedged into a smallish school desk that is itself wedged under the creaking, spider-web strewn wood of the underside of the stairs. It's so quiet here I feel like it's a big fucking joke. I have to be a character portrayed. This life has simply *got* to be written. All of everything I do is really just one big fucking joke, little set-ups, one after the other. Waking up in the morning seems like one of the more synchronized ones, it has a pattern, and because of all the alcohol my blood floats through, it feels like getting stabbed in the belly every morning I try to lift myself off the bed without wincing. A sharp pang in my belly, then the screaming muscles in my back, then the swimming head.

Somewhere in the air, roaming – somewhere – I know there's the ghost of a dead man laughing. There has to be an audience for something this delightless. Either that or I'm not getting the joke supposedly not being told. I peer out one of the pasty yellow windows of the bell tower, out across a wide expanse of burnt grass. I went to jail once and nothing I did there seemed half as useless as what I do here, like getting up, trying every morning to avoid those familiar roller-coaster drops and aching spirals. Like a big fucking joke. I was healthier in jail. And I was only in there for a week.

The business degree that enabled me after months of not getting a job to finally land a reputable one mopping dark stone floors in an unpopular museum off the beaten path of a worn highway off-ramp, is also one of the better comic strips that told my life story pretty well in the small section of irascible scenes that seem to say a whole lot with just a few shitty bubbles of dialog hovering over a picturesque me, scratching at my forehead in the damply lit foyer of the museum, getting to the big picture that is, well, what the hell am I doing? I get paid every two weeks. Tonight I'll clean up a soda spill, or something like that and I'll see payment for this menial act in *two weeks*. What if I die in *four days*?

I still have a ring on my finger, too. Not that I was ever engaged to be married. That's a bit of a stretch, even in drunk dreams. No, I *found* this fucking ring at the museum. The way I figured it, the life-changing notion that was probably slaved at to chisel a physical affection out of sentiment, resulting in the purchasing of this ring, well that good fortune will always be around even when the ring is not, for those two. Somebody lost the ring, somehow, and I found it. And not thinking, I slipped the thing on. Funny, but it wouldn't come off.

Too embarrassed to say something to somebody about what I'm doing trying on a wedding band that doesn't belong to me, I just hold my hand in my jacket pocket most days. Somewhere out there, somebody's probably got a new ring on to replace the one that I can't take off. And because the resolution has to be stronger than the loss, that ring'll be *better* than this fucking one, bear-trapping my hand. Somewhere out there, that new, better ring is reflecting the distant image of me, tucked away at this desk at the bottom of a stairwell in a bell tower, watching dust motes fall from a Heavenward distance way up the center of the tower, like they are all afraid of getting stuck on the ledge of those go-nowhere steps, leading up as they always do, to a silent, rusted bell. Filaments of rotting wood and fragments of yesterday's solidity deteriorated, traveling from a useless height, burying the past, and I just walk over it every day.

On the desk there's a postcard I've made out lovingly to this girl who works the counter at the electric company. They turned off the power here at the bell tower and I met her when I caught a taxi cab – ditching it four blocks from the power station because I couldn't actually meet the fare, even one block's passage. She looked older than me, but not by too many years. Though she certainly didn't look old. In fact, I was kind of surprised at how I felt when I realized, why am I puzzling over this girl's age? I don't feel old. Is it just that hard to look at somebody who's not, well, *useless*? The girl at the counter had a smile on her face that I don't think was an act. That smile left, of course, the minute I started crying openly, unintentionally. About the lights at the bell tower.

'That old bell tower?' she'd asked, smirking. The smirk was an act, because it was sarcastic. Not real mirth. It temporarily replaced the smile. That is, until pity took over the smirk.

'That old bell tower is where I live . . . *Cindy.*' Trying my all at being convincing, I figured I'd read the name off the placard at the front of the counter. *Melodrama gets power turned on,* I figured. Or better yet, *I can't believe I'm actually Crying.* I wondered then if I could actually feel more pity for her having to sit through this than she must have certainly felt for me having to do this for some unknown reason. I mean . . . crying?

And you know, hey, I'd get around to paying the damned bill, just like always, but not, like, right *now.* 'Cindy, I *mop floors.* In the dark, even, most of the time, because it's a shitty museum and they don't keep the lights on most of the time because they don't want to make my job even *remotely* tolerable.' I suddenly felt like an asshole for saying that. 'Wait, they don't do it to piss me off. That's not what I'm saying. They just, well they turn the lights after midnight, most of them anyway, to save on electricity. And so I have to mop floors *in the dark.* And well, I can't *do that* all night and then go home to even *more* darkness.'

'Your home is . . . that bell tower?'

'Yes. That Bell Tower. It's mine. I mean, I rent it, but it's where I live. And it's . . . *fucking dark.*'

Her face softened. I winced because it meant I was really this guy here and it wasn't some other guy playing me, but *me.* She frowned. Some of it, I guess, was due to the pity routine at once seeming so surreal, because though I was kind of acting, I also kind of wasn't. Actually, I wasn't acting, at all. I really was that pathetic. And to suddenly note that I was *playing* the part of me, *acting* out the little steps of the character that was actually me, boy did that hit hard. And I started crying like a drunk homeless person.

It was at that point that I learned never to underestimate the power of reality.

Point being, the shitty little bulb in the desk lamp lighting this crappy postcard. Well, it's *lit* now.

So I'm writing Cindy a thank-you postcard. It's something I lifted from the museum gift shop. It depicts an old cowboy with a revolver, aiming it at some bandit with a black ribbon tied around his face and eye holes cut into the fabric, loosely drawn, like the artist was drunk, commissioned with whiskey shots. It's the poorest of poor, but astoundingly the best of the postcards in that damned gift shop. But to tell you the truth . . . I was pretty drunk myself when I lifted that postcard, so there's a good chance I fucked up after all and stole the ugliest of the bunch. Though I should try to get that out of my head, because I'm trying here to do something less like a big unfavorable fuck-up and more like a rational endeavor. It isn't like me to risk my job stealing, either, especially on account of worthless pieces of artless scenic register that costs, at best, what, like fifteen cents? Is crap like this even jotted down in the inventory logs? Kids come in and out of that pointless museum all week, all of them angry and bored, wondering why their family is the only family dumb enough to get off the highway to see *this*. Some good-for-nothing house of history depicting the settlement of a town nobody even knew existed until this museum said it did. The restrooms are undoubtedly the only saving grace here for unawares travelers. And these kids, they must steal shit all the time. Postcards, hard candy, the rubber doorstops on the entry gates I keep having to replace every other day.

Funny that I puzzle over this postcard like I've committed a crime. Funny that crime can even be an action. What's crime to one person is an act of penance for another, a slip of the mind to somebody else. A drunken fuck-up to the person that only dwells on it after the fact, sitting like a dust mote under a creaky staircase in a rotting bell tower that is in worse shape than a worm-eaten casket shoved six feet under and forgotten.

I look down at the postcard and I notice I've actually asked Cindy out on a date. This blows my mind. Certain passages from the single paragraph of horribly crabbed child-scrawls:

Remember me from the service disruption at the bell tower?

I noticed you're not married.

What's it like working for the power company? Do you get paid holidays?

Staring at the postcard – there's ink spatters dotting the whole left side of the entry field because the fountain pen I wrote this with is splintered and spits out ink when you curl the pen on inward loops – I wonder what the hell is wrong with me. I can't send this.

I can't send this pile of shit.

What's worse, even – if things can get any worse – I wrote this all on a *postcard*. I didn't even have the decency – or embarrassment – to write a note I could hide from her co-workers, tucked into a private envelope. Am I to expect she'd be the only person to read this postcard, simply because it's addressed to her? This is silly. I'm dead drunk at the bottom of the stairwell. The sun is sliding in across the floor, painting the dusty floorboards gold. There's a snake worming its way along the wall at the foot of the stairs like it's scared to get too close to the middle of the room only to find it's a vortex of uselessness. It's crawling away from me, disappearing from sight. It could have been slithering around me all this time, for all I know. The new shirt I just got from the Chancellery is rather tight. I'm choking, the collar button is so tight. I'm sweating, trying to remember what Cindy really looked like in the first place. In my head I'm seeing so many faces. People I vaguely remember from college, girls I must have seen in magazines, guards from that week in jail on a drunken charge of operating a motor vehicle. All these faces and none of them are Cindy. Some of them are even just dog's heads, stuck up on the splintered tips of baseball bats and planted into the ground like corn stalks. I'm seeing rainbows in my head from after the storms. I'm seeing clouds in the sky shaped like werewolves.

This postcard is the stupidest thing I have ever done outside the guise of attempting to be a real person, no doubt about it. Crumbling it, tearing it up, stomping pieces of it into the golden orange floorboards, I see that snake again, still crawling along the inside of the floor molding on the wall opposite me, trying to find a way out.

I wish I could find a way out.

PLEASE DON'T LEAVE ME

dear
shipwreck

School had let out early again because two more bomb threats were called in to the main office. The day before that, there were two as well, which resulted in the same makeshift early day not a kid in town didn't holler and hoot for. Everyone from students to teachers to parents knew that the calls were a hoax, but by law you can't have children in a building that gets bomb threats, because it isn't safe for kids to be around bombs. The way I figured, thinking about it like a dream as the intercom in the classroom interrupted something about humpbacked whales to let us know we were free to go, was, well, what if the calls were placed *everyday*? Huh, what were they going to do? So the phones rang in the front office a lot, that month. As far as anyone was concerned, summer was starting rather early.

On my way out of the building, I spat up at the fire alarm over the exit door, thinking to myself that it was so strange how procedure worked.

So I hopped on my bike and off I went.

Since we got out before eleven, I still had my lunch money in hand, which served me well at Durwood's, a spider-webbed, checker-board floor diner where the soda bar was always over-crowded with fattened truckers and meat plant butchers all hulking over the swivel stools pouring liters of coffee down their meaty throats and talking trash about The Wife. At Durwood's, it was dirty and dark and not much fun since the pinball machine would be conceptually broken year-round and the waitresses were old and ugly enough to be truckers' mothers. But the star attraction for kids spilling out of the school wasn't ever the shining models of our future that the clientele represented, but rather that at Durwood's, they poured the single best chocolate milkshakes ever.

The skies had been storming all week, but for the first time all day the clouds let up. Some of the dampness dried up with it and I had sunshine on my face, all the way home. Milkshakes and sunlight and no school seemed more to me like a prisoner's last meal before an execution, being perfect no matter how crappy it could possibly turn out. After the first sip, in my head there was a banner-plane up in the sky spelling out: What Could Possibly Go Wrong On A Day Like This?

With my parents off at work, there would be no doubt that the doors would all be locked and double-bolted. As parents, they often prided themselves on being more caring than *other kids'* parents and as such refused to give me a key to the house, with the frame of mind that a child my age shouldn't be living an adult's life, going about as he pleases with no adult supervision, regarding kids who made their own food and let themselves in and out of the house as suffering from parental neglect. So because they loved me So Much, I didn't have a key to the house. Which resulted in me wandering the streets on days like this. Because I had nowhere to go.

The irony of their virtues used to get me really pissed, especially as it was rare I'd actually get a chance to catch the week-day soaps with those awful actresses who happened to usually appear on screen half-naked, at least once per episode.

But it was too good a day to waste pitching a fit. Besides, I thought I might catch Cory on the way out soon enough, anyway.

He was my unemployed older brother who probably wouldn't open the door to let me in even if there were wolves outside. Not even Cory could get me down on such a perfect day, though. So I sat cross-legged on the porch out of the way of the front hall windows – so Cory couldn't see me sitting out there and thus attempt an exit out the back of the house, just to be an asshole – and sipped from my milkshake, which was still cold and still thick after twenty something minutes of slightly damp yet passionately rough February sunshine.

Sipping on that shit like I was worth my weight in it, pondering the glorious day, that's when I noticed Boil Corpon across the street, climbing up onto his bike, which was always left propped up against the front porch railing since because he was a small little kid he needed to climb it to get on. Pretty much everyone on the block was probably still in the vicinity of school save for myself and Boil. It practically felt like we were alone in the neighborhood *together*. I shivered at the thought of being lumped into whatever Boil was doing. Feeling like he was my only company was not something I wanted to dwell on. Not in the presence of such a perfect chocolate milkshake. Not on a bomb threat day.

Boil was a nickname that the kid had acquired years previous, because he'd developed some kind of condition that made his skin puff up into sad-looking blisters, kind of like a large snake with arms, legs, and hives. It confounded me that his mother would ever let him go out on sunny days with a skin condition like that. Wouldn't excessive sunlight pop him like a cream-filled balloon? Maybe she was still in bed, with the curtains typically drawn tight, assuming it was still rainy out, giving Boil the okay to go outside to play.

Boil Corpon, whose birth name was Corpon Eleanor, was younger than me and most of my friends by two grades, although he wasn't actually in school like the rest of us anymore. He'd been removed from regular school just as soon as that eerie skin condition became, somehow, permanent. My parents were decent enough neighbors to the Eleanors, but if they ever knew exactly what it was that Boil had, such information was never once hinted at, in my presence. Probably they thought I would tell all the kids in the neighborhood. And probably they were dead right.

It's bad enough the kids tease him anyway, my mom would say.

What she didn't understand was that Boil was something unfinished and repulsive that should never have been born in the first place, regardless of whatever sickness he'd just recently contracted. Apocalyptic ailments weren't going to make that easy to overlook. But still, my mother would play the guardian and I was always the culprit of some crime for just looking at the kid.

One time during a covered-dish luncheon after the church service, I'd referred to him by the forbidden nickname within a very proximate hearing distance of the kid's parents and one of *my* parents – I don't recall which – slapped me without saying a word as to why. At the time, these were two separate incidences to me. It wasn't until much later in the afternoon, when my face was still burning, that I figured out why. And as one could guess, I was surely very hateful of Boil that day. But I guess what he had must have been pretty horrible if the lid was shut that tight on it, so even though I hated the kid, I figured I had the slap coming to me, so I dealt with it and fucking forgot about Boil.

Leaning back against the garage door, forsaking my spot under the porch windows since it was such a beautiful day, I sat in the sun and sipped and watched the blistery snake kid fumble about like an idiot trying to mount the bicycle.

So Boil fell off the bike the first time he tried getting on, of course, and the second try too, but landed a *starring role* in success when remounting over and over again like a true dumb champion. I was still of the mind, however, that he was a complete failure anyway, with or without a body bubbled in blisters, and that far from just a minor series of incidents, getting on that bike over and over again until he didn't fall the fuck over again was like a metaphor for his entire life: There's nothing else to do, so keep doing that.

He rode around in circles a little bit by the garage before pulling out of the loop to make the descent down the driveway. Noticing me watching him, he waved.

I flipped Boil Corpon the bird.

Boil looked ready to fall from his bike again, eyes bulging and his tongue lolling out, seemingly pretty damned scared. He made a quick turn and looped back up the driveway, as if he were going to scuttle back inside the house, throwing his eyes back over his shoulder at me, still staring. I suspected that even if he didn't have such a disgusting skin condition everyone would still poke fun at a kid that ugly.

Once at the garage again, Boil wheeled his bike back around, picking his ass up off the seat while leaning his whole body forward to put more weight on the pedals. And then out of the blue, he shot back down the embankment of the driveway, staring right at me with that wild, bug-eyed glare of his. I removed the cool milkshake from my sight just long enough for Boil to make his demonic skin condition descent down the driveway, half thinking that little outpatient bastard might actually be trying to wheel up the front of my driveway and slam right into me.

But that didn't happen, at all. Not even close. Instead, Boil made a wide left as he hit the street separating my half of the neighborhood from his. The front tire shook a little bit as he raised his fist at me, sputtering in a cracked voice not used to talking much '*I'm telling on you!*' And then he disappeared off down the street behind some dead fruit trees and a row of hedges lining the sidewalk, well out of my sight.

But I was hardly given the time to suggest to myself that little Boil Corpon had a lot more than just medical complications setting him back from fitting in with the kids at school, when I heard a loud crash, followed by a deafening pop, from behind the fruit trees. Seconds later, three speeding objects came flying down the street from the direction Boil had darted off into, each traveling at practically the same speed and two of them in mid-air.

The first was a rusted white pick-up with the logo of *Five Bright Stars Roofing* painted and peeling on the side of the driver's door. That was what caught my attention first, because it was so big and white. But then I saw the two other things racing like jets, hovering a few feet over the truck just like jets would.

It was Boil's lime green bicycle. And also Boil.

The roofing pick-up eventually screeched to a halt as it pushed through the Eleanor's front yard and slammed into the side of the house. Pretty much exactly as that happened, Boil and the bike came down hard and hit the street a few dozen feet from the house, tumbling and skidding like bags of mulch across the asphalt, tearing open like bags of mulch would.

And just as suddenly as the clamor had erupted, it was all over.

Boil Corpon looked like a dog that just got hit by a car, only he was a boy that only sort of kind of looked like a dog. The roofer stumbled out of the crumpled truck as bricks from the equally destroyed Eleanor house avalanched over him like rain and fittingly, as I suspected he would, he collapsed into the grass, motionless.

Mrs. Eleanor practically broke through the front door screen, half screaming *Oh My God!* with noticeable confusion and pretty heart-felt horror. When her eyes hit upon the mess in the street, which included a lime green tangle of steel and split rubber tires, she shrieked so loud I thought my eyes would pop.

I'd already begun walking toward where Boil lay, so I made it to the edge of my driveway by the time Mrs. Eleanor fell down on her knees by her son. She reached down and scooped him up, hugging his leaking body to her chest like a popped water balloon still seeping fluid. Some of it was his blood, but the rest of it was either from his torn stomach or whatever it was that filled those awful sores canvassing his body like such a crude oil painting.

But all that was just average stuff.

Everybody reads the newspaper, so everyone's aware that bad things happen. Now what *really* made me remember this whole scene after so many years is what happened as I was just about to walk back up to the porch, in the hopes that Cory would come running to see what all the commotion was about and I could then finally get in the house and lock *him* out. That notion – that hurried plan – completely left my mind once I saw Boil's gorgeous sister Katie Anne come lurching out of the house in nothing but a skimpy black bra and some really, really tight corduroy shorts cut-off nearly at the waistline. It stopped me as dead in my tracks as Boil was.

My eyes just practically shot right out of my head, bullets from the shotgun of my skull echoing down the street like Mrs. Eleanor's cries were doing.

Katie Anne Eleanor was Cory's age and I think that lucky louse had even fucked her once a few years ago, but he'd not have opened up to me about something like that even if I'd just miraculously – or surgically – regained my hearing after a struggled life of deafness. Cory had always been an asshole and I don't think these kinds of things mellow with age.

But that's old news. What was really burning in my veins was how a faultless girl such as Katie Anne – tall, thin, looked like a jeans model, half naked, crying her eyes out, causing my heart to skip and murmur – could possibly be physically related to a virtual family tumor like Boil. It was just incredible to me. And it perplexed me ever much more than the thought of my brother possibly getting to sleep with her did. I had never been one to question nature too deeply, though, finding it better to just accept majesty when it bites you in the eyes, so I let the mystery step aside for the moment, hoping Katie Anne would jump up off the street and run in to call an ambulance. If that happened, I'd watch her chest the whole way, I declared.

And I did get to do that, after a time.

But for a long while, it seemed, Katie Anne just knelt there on the blood-drenched pavement, sobbing out leagues of salty tears that I wanted to taste. Her face was red and her hair a mess as she coughed and choked on tears in the grass by the easement when Mrs. Eleanor stood up and Boil's head fell back so far that I could hear what was left of his neck give in and snap. Mrs. Eleanor screeched, but never let go of Boil the entire time.

I'll never forget the image of Katie Anne that day, though. That moment in time – twelve years of age and wiser than I'd ever want to be – was when I opened my eyes and realized just how attractive girls could be when they were crying.

Our family was invited to the funeral and I desperately wanted to see what Katie Anne looked like in a black dress, standing by the coffin. But my mother had forced me to stay home with Cory, who, by the way, didn't come out of his room all morning, not even when I twisted my ankle and tumbled down the stairs into the bedroom hall, unable to move, wailing like a puppy dog only a few feet from his door.

along the poor,
darling way

The beginning of the morning was a litany of howls, but by noon we were listening to a softly bitter but hushed wind brushing through the trees in the vast apple orchard we were technically rather lost in. It hadn't been planned as such a long stay here in the orchard, but it's so much of a winding, hilly ordeal that when coupled with casks of rum and wine, we found that it was not quite as difficult as it would seem to become lost.

It would, of course, be an easy enough task to find the fence if we'd only felt like it to walk long enough. But here in the orchard, it was not simply a matter of tracing your way back with bread crumbs and you had to be careful about attracting attention that close to the woods, because if you were spotted, you might never get a chance to reclaim posture away from that. It could mean the abrupt end of your life. Above the orchard, looking around in any direction, there are no sentinels of land – like a mountain or even some agonizingly tall, lonely willow tree – by which to gauge the way that would be north or which might become south, the opposite direction of town. And the howls all around us at night and certain parts of the day were telling only of a dizzying nature as far as where *they* were coming from. We could be anywhere, here.

All the reasonable reasons can also be combined with another bundle of more salient facts, these ones personal, namely that Shannon and I weren't terribly bothered to find our way through the orchard just yet, anyway. Not really looking for a section maybe out of harm's way in the rickety circumference of the fence that would allow us enough time to wander not too indirectly back toward the safety of the town. Tired of making plans, the two of us inadvertently planned on shrugging regular things off – like *safety* or the *future*.

Figuring the everlasting wealth of marvelously green apples dangling in front of our faces all the live-long day would be grounds enough to avoid starvation or even mild hunger, we'd brought along with us alcohol as our sustenance of choice to wait out the time between us, the woods and – if it should really come down to it – a search party. But we'd had it in mind to spend some time together away from the rest of the world, or as it happens, just in some frighteningly lonesome other one.

True, if the worst of it came into play, we could still scream our lungs out and perhaps somebody nearer the town might hear us then and have a go at barging through the woods with fire and guns. But that way too, proclaiming for all the angels in Heaven '*Here We Are!*' so perfectly naked like that, the probability of a rogue creature scaling the fence and reaching us first was too great. Nobody really knows what it is about the orchard that could possibly ward off the creatures, the werewolves, but in any case, it's been only hastily tested – some kids here, some kids there, some loose horses – and nobody's been attacked directly within its fences thus far – no horses or humans or even apple trees destroyed. And I'm so drunk and despondently aloof half the time that even a slightly sarcastic idea can be taken pretty damned far. And anyway, we are both recent college drop-outs with no jobs and nothing to do but hang out in a fairly dangerous apple orchard outside the pitchforks, loaded shotguns, and burning torches of the town.

Shannon's way of putting it – when we'd first hopped the fence and left a blazing trail of rum spilled from open bottles as we tore into the orchard's shadows and apples – was 'Who gives a fuck about werewolves?'

And I know this is hardly the definitive way to look at it, but weeks ago the sudden, muscle-defying look on her father's face when she told him right in front of me that'd we'd both decided to drop out together, that kind of untold rage was enough to know that lycanthropy is not the be-all-end-all of violence. I could tell he was close to hitting her – and probably he did, later – but with me standing there, I guess he felt such means to an end might be just a bit mistimed. It's easy to get tired of that. Sometimes I start to wish people like *him* would be the ones mauled in the dark hours of the night, instead of people who aren't stepping in the way of anyone else's lives. Like our two friends Linus and Lynn, paternal twins we knew from college who had dropped out a few weeks previous to us and who, not long after, were found torn to pieces in the living room of their parents' house by the ravine, where gruesome encounters had become increasingly common. That night, detectives had grimly dusted for fingerprints a wildly smashed front picture window and the nearly caved in wall around it. Silently, they'd gathered up tufts of bloody hair and then sealed them so very competently into plastic bags like this Evidence would be useful toward anything; the twins' parents couldn't even cry – they'd just stared, white-faced, at what the detectives were doing, or what they could possibly *think* they were doing. And here we are now, amidst all this fucking carnage and sadness, somehow supposed to be of the notion that dropping out of college can wreck one's life. It's easy to get tired of that.

In the orchard, the fencing itself is about as low to the ground as a puppy dog on its hind legs, so it's not a matter of scaling this perimeter that keeps the werewolves at bay. Not that any physical barriers of some stronger or more threatening kind could stop their rampages much, anyway. They just plain don't come here. Whatever the cause may be for their unwillingness to come into the orchard, we've been sleeping here for two nights and though we hear them quite clearly in the darkness, waiting for us, and even occasionally as we glimpse them off behind the fences when the sun retreats behind cloud cover and the drizzle begins, it's like this place could rightly burn them to the touch or something.

I guess we're either lucky or out of our minds. As for me, it's both. Lucky that I'm here. With her. Alone. And the latter because I've come here. With her. *Alone.*

Shannon's dressed for the most part in the same thing she's been wearing for days. The pale brown fabric of her dress is littered with falling yellow flowers that match the falling yellow of her eyes, and up along the low cut that just manages to cling to the swell of her chest, the flowers here are embroidered with string and lace, and half green. Over this – but still shivering slightly in the drizzle of the rain – a dark brown cardigan sweater with light brown sleeve cuffs that match in color the soft waterfall of hair spilling over her shoulders, shimmering in the partial could-be storm, rusted a peachy brown – the shade the flesh of an apple will turn when it's been exposed to the air too long.

I'm winding the frames of film as she reaches up to cup her palm behind an apple that's suspended just above her head and with a switchblade in her other hand she pierces it straight through, slowly, and the clicks of the camera worm around the tight little smile her mouth forms. The gently turning eyes are large and demure as she peers almost secretly not in the direction of the camera lens, but at my one visible eye gazing out from behind it at her. Releasing the handle of the knife and lowering a hand to her waistline, resting it on her hip in an overwhelmingly

89

cute way I can't seem to take my eyes from, turning her face smoothly, nonchalantly, so that her chin aims slightly toward one shoulder, she drops down into a cute, graceful curtsy that pulls her other hand just slightly out of reach from cupping the pierced apple, and it swings away from her precisely as the hair on her shoulders pushes forward when she bows. With one hand slightly open-palmed, offered toward the camera in a small wave before grasping the hem of her skirt, her curtsy falls even lower and the apple is no longer in the frame. Two or three frames later, it's just the top of her dress, her shoulders and the prioritized saintly elegance of her face. And then, after I shoot my reflection in her sparkling eye, I lower the camera, lean in to kiss her, and she laughs a little, quietly, and we hear high-pitched howls responding from deep within the woods, stretching into a furtive echo through the trees like a breeze.

A rumble from the atmosphere is the promise of a long, wet afternoon. And so after another roll of film, settling on an ending shot of her discarded sweater – the sleeve-cuff lying handless in the grass snaking around a discarded but well-placed apple Shannon's taken a sizeable, exaggerated bite out of – we walk together back toward our tent – which takes us a few minutes to find. We drink sour rum from a full-brimmed tin cup until the bottle is empty, and we curl up under a single blanket, my arm around her warm shoulders and my chin underneath where her ear hides the soft slope of the top of her neck. Then we fall asleep and it's almost dark by the time either of us opens our eyes again.

It's probably the lull of the rain as it dots the tent above our eyes, but it provokes the same reaction in me that it does in Shannon, and we are both entranced. The droplets, thousands of them, poke effortlessly against the vinyl, and not piercing it, they all give up immediately upon contact, skittering along in short trails of aimless wandering until they join up with other droplets in previously devised rivulets, and then, feeling confident in that way, the thin streams trail down the side of the tent and disappear into the shadows where the waning sun isn't so keen on chasing them.

A well of deep thunder like a barreling stagecoach wheels its way around the orchard, roaring past us to terrorize some other part of the area as it still terrorizes us in its wake, and I am taken out of the trance, sitting up, shivering, feeling distinctly uneasy. Shannon grasps my leg, but she's still staring up at the outlines of the raindrops canvassing the top of the tent. Eventually she sits up, too.

She's cold, so I bundle her up in my ratty green pullover and we go out in search of the sweater we'd absent-mindedly abandoned earlier in the day while drinking and kissing.

The uneasy feeling in me gets stronger and seems like it's pulling fiercely at my stomach lining like a fish hook. The stronger it tugs in that direction, I somehow know to follow it that way and move so that it doesn't tug so hard. And sickeningly, when this happens Shannon holds tighter to my arm, like she feels it, too. The air smells not just damp, but dirty.

Like wet animals.

The cardigan – when we find it – is still where the apple is, only in *worse* shape than the apple now and scattered in pieces all around us, like it was used as confetti. I drop the tin cup of wine we were sharing sips from and it splashes deep red over the grass, the rotting green apple with the bite taken from it, and the myriad tatters of the cardigan that looks, too, like it's had a bite – or bites – taken from it.

So I know we are fools, her and I. Or at least me. Yeah, it's definitely me.

After all, it was *my* sweetly importunate suggestions that probably swayed her in the first place to actually go along with this outrightly shitty and really stupid plan to penetrate woods no one should be messing around in. This carnivorously stupid plan of mine to spend a few nights in a deserted apple orchard haunted by the constant presence of surrounding creatures that will not hesitate to tear us apart in the same way the sweater's been.

Why do things happen? I think momentarily of how happy I've been since coming here with her. How different I feel in just two days. It's only now that I realize, despite the inherent danger of what we were actually doing, being with her is stronger than fear, and with a certain inner sense of adoration that truly borders on liberation, I can recall every drunken click of the camera and every frame she's wandered in and out of, every moment of eye contact, and I can see the swirls of nameless beauty and color it would become on print, runny with saturated yellows and burned oranges and all the times here I thought I was doing the right thing, for once in my life.

I look at all that like two people who don't want to change the entire world can change a small part of theirs, if only they do it together. And on the surface, that seemed slightly heroic. Or could even be construed as some sort of rebellious lack of sympathy for personal harm that heroism is based upon. But even though it could be all those things and more in some fluently lacking and botched punchline, overall what it really is – stronger than anything – is just plain stupidity on my part. I'm so drunk and confused I can barely make out right from wrong, yet standing here holding Shannon I know I've just done the worst thing I could have done to her. *Because more than likely, neither of us is going to escape this silly orchard.* This non-enchanted orchard. This apple field that just fucking *exists.*

'What the hell is this shit?' she whispers, her large eyes wide as holes in the earth not even a canyon could hide in, glaring along with me at slashed fragments of her soaked and demolished sweater. These werewolves don't just destroy things, they erase them from comprehensible existence. They tear them apart. Whatever it is that's not allowing them to turn back into something safer, it's filled with rage and they tear everything in their path to tiny bits and pieces. Especially those things which are alive. Such as things like Shannon and I.

'I don't even know what to say,' I recognize out loud.

'Is someone playing a joke on us?' she asks, hoping, looking over her shoulder, an ineffectual action which gets me looking around, too. But the air smells more thickly now of wet fur, because we know exactly what it is we smell. All of a sudden, we are spinning back-to-back in dizzying circles, but all we discover is rain, apple trees, and orange beams from a rapidly setting – disappearing – sun. That nobody came here to spook us is a very uncompromising fact, cold like headstone cement. It's not a joke someone is playing. The sweater littering the ground all around us isn't a fabricated act.

One of them has come into the orchard.

At *least* one of them, anyway. But that's not any consolation. However many of them are actually here means nothing in the long run, because *one* is all it takes. I didn't bring a gun. Shannon brought a switchblade, but what's *that* going to do? Really, what would a gun do for us now, either? I've never fired a gun before and I'm pretty sure Shannon hasn't used one either, so we'd probably have to be pretty close to that fucking massive, growling thing to hope one of the bullets would hit it where it would count. And the closer you get to one of those things, the worse your chances are of getting away again – if you've any chance at all. It usually takes a *whole group* of petrified gun-slingers – high on lead poisoning from filling silver bullet casings – to take down a single one of these things. So what's a couple of drunk kids like us going to effect even *if* we had something like a gun to Protect us?

We walk quietly back to the tent. And holding her tight, not making a sound, we huddle underneath the blanket, shivering. I feel really, really bad. I feel awful. But I tense up and act like it's not too much of a big deal, with the hope of affecting the perceivable notion that I can handle this.

But I can't handle this. And really what I am thinking is that I am the worst person Shannon has ever met.

fall
down, anatomy

I

At the department store I'm standing in, along the aisle I'm standing in, right in front of me, stretching fully eight or more feet in either direction, are hung on the rack dozens of heavy white coats patterned with arrangements of flowers and oranges.

My wife, Deborah May, in her time had once an immense love for fabric patterns like this. She owned innumerable dresses, shirts, linens, and everything else, bearing bouquets of flowers and baskets of oranges. During our fourteen year marriage, I'd presented her with countless such articles of clothing, donned with prints anywhere from bunches of water lilies tied delicately with string, copious crates of falling oranges pouring from the heavens, to evenly spaced rows of bright yellow sunflowers. Admittedly, my sense of fashion was never something one might refer to as impressive and in my days did find my poorly managed way into a few purchases I'd initially been quite stricken by only to discover upon presenting them to Deborah May as gifts that her eyes were drifting from the prints on the dresses to the wall, silent.

At those times, I wondered why a lady like her had been with me at all. Or why we were still together, after so many years. What a man like me was doing with her.

It wasn't that we didn't get on well with one another. We *did*. Too well, probably, considering our various uncontested contrasts. It was probably our ability to remain satisfied that we were so uncommon in our various likes and dislikes that made us such a *lasting* couple, because for what little we eventually had in common, our greatest connection of all was that neither of us exhibited much motive, and this was such a strong, unspoken thing between the two of us that it formed a bond neither of us had much desire to disturb. There were, of course, the more trivial differences and disagreements no more argumentative than those of most any other couple – though one facet of our relationship was, in particular, of a grave importance I never fully grasped until it was too late … But I think I had actually stopped loving her only three or four years into our marriage.

For her, I think she might have felt the same. Otherwise, why was it made so unproblematic to not love one another yet still find ourselves willing to carry on the marriage, as if the fact did not matter? Or at least this is what I believe was the case, looking back on everything. We just didn't have anything else planned for the horizon, is how best to say it if having to speak on behalf of the two of us, for we'd nowhere else to go but home to each other. And so it was with this quiet and complacent manner that our marriage, though lasting and otherwise prolonged, simply *existed*.

If ever the matter did sneak into a conversation, it was almost as if by accident. And recognizing its existence, I suppose it was politely dropped. And courteous as we were raised, so droll, too. We said little to nothing about anything important – this thing at the back of our minds, or anything else. Marriage meant finality for the two of us, it seemed to me. A place to notch on a doorway's threshold like the precipitous heightening of a child. Once done, always forevermore, and to the history books with that.

This is what I am thinking about at present, as I wander the lonely shopping aisle, picking through a section of soft white jackets with honey bees and oranges tangled in thin green vines down the sleeves.

II

Last month would have been our fifteenth anniversary. I'd bought a crystal vase for her and had it stuffed with sunflowers; I placed the vase atop her gravestone in Merry Park a week or so late of the anniversary. It doesn't really seem to matter to me that I'm late with an anniversary gift, because she's dead, but it was there for me to see upon visiting her that many immediate family members had of course been to my wife's grave to leave their gifts – all of these presents lovely but so sorrowful – in much more punctual a fashion than I. And more likely than not, too, also noting that nothing seemed, visibly, to have been left by me. That can't look too certainly moving in aid to their views of me, whatever those views may be.

A thief will inevitably take the crystal vase. I know this. Quietly in the night, maybe. Or even in daylight hours. What's the difference?

It makes no difference to me.

Christmas is only days away, now and the department store is packed but for this aisle alone, which I am glad for. Which is why I've been standing here perusing coats for the better part of an hour. All in all, this is why I haven't left yet. Because I can't look at anybody, right now. They'll see my face pinkish with wet streaks glistening under my eyes from the crying. I don't really know why I've been crying, either. Which makes it all the more unbearable.

I think in some ways I did still love Deborah May. Or else why *should* I be crying?

We were by no means the best of friends but we were, more or less, close to one another. We'd still slept in the same bed. Pleasantries were exchanged formally in small pockets of commonplace regularity yet with considerably moderate honesty: before breakfast, the early morning minutes preceding parting for work, shaving time in the mirror, sharing meaningless good-nights before extinguishing the light in bed at night and so on the next day, one after the other. My, for a decade.

In July, I lay her to rest. The wake held had been carried out for the betterment of weeping family under a closed casket, but when the congregation had thronged out into the parking lot, left alone with her I'd lifted the top section of the lid and then quietly I said good-bye to her, without crying. She was dressed reverently, beautifully in white, which had been her favorite color.

There were no patterns on the burial dress.

And I remember very distantly that I told her 'Thank you,' but I don't remember if I had a reason for doing so or what I meant by saying it.

I think perhaps it was because I was appropriately at a loss for words.

III

In August, my twin brother James was convicted of the murder of Deborah May Garden.

During the few proceedings I was physically if not wholly in emotional attendance for, James looked in my direction not once. Me, however, well I stared at him the entire damned time. My eyes, when court let out, would feel blistered and dry, cracked as winter lips. I'd stared at him until the air conditioning vents were like razor blades to my raw pupils. The deep, dark resentment I'd felt for him had its fingers buried in the soft flesh over my skull, training my head toward my twin brother, even at those times I'd felt the eyes would melt in my head. The profound shock and disgust writhing in me bore resemblance to a giant snake in its deathbed, shedding scales as it hissed in rapid spurts, coiling. How my innards squirmed and boiled in the throes of that hate. I'd wondered aloud at times – much to the chagrin of James' lawyer – what my brother was then thinking. Causing, simultaneously, both calamity and hushes.

Divulgence to any reason for his actions there was none. Nor did the testimony ever writhe with hints as to the trial getting any nearer to that answer. As to why he'd one day taken a heavy bit of wood to my wife while she'd slept an afternoon quietly by, alone in the den while I was away at work, there was quite plainly no information forthcoming. No answer.

No detected signs of struggle were determined, moving investigators to agree Deborah May had died never knowing her death. At once sleeping, then simply gone.

The courtroom on these days seemed to me filled gracelessly with skeletons. Every bleacher packed, every table guarded, every wall lined with skeletons dressed in flat gray suits, buzzing like flies in the lifeless echo of mumbles, creaking wood, shuffling papers, crossed legs, all mingling but meaning nothing. Itinerant noise. From my peripheral vision, all I could see was gray as I stared ahead, between lifeless heads propped over gray suits, toward my twin brother James, who had murdered my wife.

Sometimes through a veil of tears that threatened to break but would not, I'd blink ever so slowly and the room would be turned black when next my eyes opened. Fuzzy shapes shuffled about and moved and I hoped when I saw the world again, in focus, it would be Deborah May's eyes, living, looking at me from the other side of the bed, vanquishing the horrid dream of gavels and evidence and the blood in the air over my detestable sibling.

Walking down the courthouse steps, as other people went along their way and cars hummed by in the traffic beyond the yard, it was just another day in the world. Unable to shake the feeling that I understood very little about that world, I touched the buttons of my coat and descended the steps, saying nothing. The trial passed like just any other month in the year. It solved nothing.

Privately, only after incarceration when the papers had long forgotten this tale, James admitted to having been in love with Deborah May.

This came to me with something like a labyrinth of ways I might interpret or be expected to interpret it. Not singularly a *surprise* was this belated confession, but something close to it, choked with revulsion. Suddenly staring at blank walls left me wondering how many ways one might interpret a white coat of paint. The verdict of Guilty was just a way to screw a lid over a jar and put that jar on the shelf. But what is held in that jar is just that. Held. Preserved.

This overwhelmed me to such a degree that I did not move from my chair, until the next morning.

More shockingly than this admission, however, my twin brother came clean also concerning two *other* murders. One of these he'd said was committed the very month before he'd done the same to my wife, and the first, a full year prior to it. Both previous women, by his account, appeared unerringly in every way like Deborah May. Furthermore, he'd acknowledged with finality that this last fact was no coincidence.

I have not spoken with my brother since his arrest. Not even at the trial did we exchange words. And not after. It happened. A lid was screwed on it.

I sat on another shelf. In my own jar.

IIII

Not a few times during the slow crawl of my marriage to her did I suspect that she might have been having an affair with James. Actually, though at the time it would have shamed me to admit such mistrust in my own wife and brother, I'd thought about this scenario quite often. The signs were most certainly there, of course. Deborah May and my brother had been very close friends. Closer than her and I. Number one.

They'd regularly attended films together, dinner, tennis matches. They liked the same food, both sharing a distinct fondness for classical music and for white wines,

Where I was subdued, he was buoyant. Where I fell short of offering surprise, James had been emotively and persistently exciting. Where those might thank me for a gift, James would go deaf under the fanfare. He was my *visual* equivalent, yes, but me not in heart nor head. And if physical attraction is truly the first hook in any courtship, I might as well have just been a stepping stone to James.

But love is a many-tentacled beast. And to my privately revolted humiliation, I'd tried my best to excise my head of thoughts of her and my brother closer than more-than-friendly arm's length, with their limbs tangled together. Like they'd just tumbled down a steep mountainside, knotted together because they'd *refused* to let one another go, tied like a ribbon of human bones, but in effect, safe. I'd often dismissed the notion as petty, as typical of a man who did not feel for his own wife what he so wanted to feel, which was, very pointedly, *love*. Was mere jealousy truly why I'd often suspected my own twin brother of committing treason against me? With my wife? At the time, it seemed right to pin it all on a matter of jealousy, at which point sleep could be attained without tearing my hair out.

During the trial, there'd been no mention of any facts supporting those many fears I'd lived with, other than the prosecutor's flagrantly alluring suggestion of a love tryst, which truly pained me to hear. And this accusation, too, James vehemently denied at the time, *continuing* to do so even after his private confession as to his love for her. Open wide on both the subjects of pitiable desire and the upsetting details of Deborah May's last moments, I can see no reason to suspect he would deny having her if have her he did. He just *wanted* to.

So I took this into consideration. And for the sake of releasing some of the tension in me caused by that now remote suspicion of unfaithfulness, I've come to terms with the truth of the facts bared in court. That James and Deborah May had not slept together is something I still believe, although I don't know why I should believe in anything at all. Had I ever once suspected my brother of murder, before his unexpected arrest? Never. Of even the simplest cruelty beyond the obviously aforementioned close relationship with my wife? Not even once. In fact, up until the three of us were forever separated from one another, I'd chided myself *constantly* at the very *inhumanness* of thinking ill conduct on the part of my brother.

When all was said and done, the tug of war had been won over by faith. In friends and family.

And when Deborah May was found dead, I had not even called James to tell him, thinking it would surely break his heart. My first reaction was, as it were, a private horror, my body feeling like a funnel my disassociated head spun through and toward the black hole of. Then came revulsion, chased quickly with a short spell of appalling sickness, whereupon I nearly lost the contents of my stomach. Then a hasty, shattered voice put through to the authorities. Then a call to my mother. After all these exhausting actions, I'd put my hollowed, suddenly haunted body to bed, leaving officials and others to handle every last aspect else.

Only twice since all this happened have I spoken to Deborah May's parents. Much like my relations with co-workers, the Cheaundlers and I were never too very distant but still not truly honestly engaged with one another. Deborah May's passing did little to revert this. In fact, it worked in much the opposite way. So few words were spoken between us after the initial murder that it bordered on becoming the colloquy of complete strangers at a bus stop, effected in petite mini-plays or air-pockets of pre-fabricated condolences or fidgety small talk.

After the trial, we'd exchanged some words, understandably brief though they were.

Partly masked family shame – and one family's blame – was brought up in small hints, then promptly discarded and apologized for. This had been quite efficiently humiliating to me and no less physically hurtful as well, as it gave me pains in my spine the likes of which falling from the ledge of a skyscraper might induce.

But I didn't hold my wife's mother and father in ill regard for looking at me as the reason for their sorrow. After all, whenever her parents were so unfortunate as to picture in their weeping heads my brother beating to death their daughter, *whose face did they see* doing it? James was my physical contemporary in every way and I of course looked exactly in their minds like the murderer of their sleeping daughter. Because we're twins. That murderer and I.

If the three had ever spent time in the same room together, I could count the words spoken between them on my fingers, so I know the parents were infinitely less familiar with him as a person than they were with me. When they pictured the death of their daughter, James' face was mine and no matter how much they did or didn't try to, they pictured *me*. So how can they ever be expected to face me again, without cringing? It hurts, but I can deal with that. Because I have no choice but to.

Sometimes I can't even help myself from picturing what James did, either. And like sitting in front of a television screen, seeing myself in the act. This occurs at those increasingly unavoidable moments when I catch my own reflection in a mirror or in a pane of glass. Even when I look into the closet for a sweater and have to rummage through Deborah May's now dusty outfits, remembering how she looked wearing such articles on the very way to meet my twin brother James for lunch. It was like picturing myself with her at the café. In every way possible, every inescapable thought of what happened to her would hang my face in unbearably distinct portraiture and it chips away at my being, violently, day after day after day after day.

The features of me are ghosts of what happened.

V

Leaving the department store empty handed, I am suddenly taken by a thick streak of guilt that shoots through my head like the reverberations of a tumor and I duck into a trinkets shop, emerging moments later with a porcelain angel which I promptly have wrapped and discard it on the headstone my wife is buried under.

And I drive away from the cemetery.

With any luck, I won't ever have a reason to return.

PLEASE DON'T LEAVE ME

planting flowers in
the frost

Anymore I feel as though, rather than having *lived* my life up to this point, I've actually only just scribbled it down, the bulk of it being in a frantic rush to get it all in before particularities disappear. Accounts become fumbled, tumbling over themselves, effectively compacting to the point where it's all quite an effort to sit with. That the script is in shorthand is part of the huge problem of why it's a lost history, because I don't understand shorthand. I can't read it, so basically, when I look back on it all, it's my own lost history I'm struggling to decipher. I'm learning.

Sometimes however, there is nothing there to decipher and I can see that. Either it's lapsed time where nothing happened or – more probably – I just can't read a word of it. But I can remember small parts. Shreds peeled out. It feels like being a ghost, looking in on one moment, over and over again.

But not really.

Every so here and there I find myself incapable of remembering the awkward things, because they get wiped out a little by more recent, less detrimental memories, and I hold onto the new ones, which are, in fact, probably just ways to walk around the subject. So I suppose it s not a bad thing when I look back on it, that now it means more. Even if it didn't happen that way.

But this is all happening exactly like I think it is, which is bewildering, to say the least.

I don't struggle to get through anything, though I'm quite sure at times that the tense feeling in my stomach has a lot to do with struggling. Right now, comprehending more than I want to, I realize how small and useless I am. Standing on a sidewalk in the neighborhood, taking everything in, I feel like I could reasonably squeeze myself into a crack in the sidewalk. Towering up above me, to prove this point, an ageless tree that is encompassing the entire width of my vision, soaking through peripheral perimeters just a tiny bit in the process, is the scariest thing I can think of right now. This tree has been alive so much longer than I have. But I've been more places than it has and I've seen more of the world. I've made more decisions and I've solved more problems. Yet standing here, doing virtually nothing, I get the creeping feeling that it's done an astounding bit more in one day of its vast life than ever I could in the whole of mine. This thoroughly bothers me and begins to unravel all those supposed decisions and all those problems I'd once thought I'd solved.

I'm all alone out here on the sidewalk. There is nobody outside, because it's wet and freezing out. And the unforgiving, nearly accusatory solitude makes me wonder why I'm trying to do better than a tree. Then I grasp that this notion is merely effort on my part to try to offer an excuse for myself. It's off-putting. And I now feel terribly dizzy.

I take one last look up into the branches. Thick boughs push outward of it like great arms, taking in miles and miles with gigantic, knotted eyes right at the top of the stem where the wood starts to split. Two massive arms spreading silently, gigantic and superior. Meekly, I peer down at my cold, pink hands. These are useless claws, I sigh to myself. With effort, I gulp. And without having another look at the stationary monolith, still as death before me – doing *more*, *better*, mystifyingly *meaningful* things than I ever have – I shove my hands back into my pockets and continue the walk home. Frustration tags along, pecking at the nape of my neck. Shooing it away with my hands would make me look like I'm crazy, so I keep the hands in my pockets and try to think of anything at all besides.

In a few hours, Alice will return home to me and hopefully I will forget all of this.

Since her departure, I've been colder, more alone than ever. The emptiness in me has become an immeasurable void since she stepped out of town to attend her mother's funeral without me.

It's not a silly thing to miss somebody this much, especially considering the alternative to being with her – this terrible, isolated frustration. And it took me this short yet draining week to realize that without her I simply do not exist. It's caused a hollow rift that has yet to show signs of a measurable depth, and I agonize for her return in justly pitiful ways, beckoning a sealant to this yawning loneliness.

Coming to depend on somebody for contentment does not feel as pathetic as it would otherwise sound to me if I'd have heard it coming from someone else's mouth, in line at a supermarket or something. Anything I was before her has been made insignificant and though I still think I mean nothing *with* her, I let the shaking pass, disregard it regally and take her word for it. And I don't question it. And I enjoy the love and the trust, the friendship and the mere *proximity* of Alice. This girl that stepped literally into my life one unassuming day when it fell upon my duty as a citizen to escort her across the road on a rainy Christmas afternoon, amidst a sea of traffic.

At Pill's Haberdashery, I push a quarter across the bar and Old Arnold – who has been employed here since it was owned by Pill and had still specialized in men's ties – pushes back a few dimes and a nickel. I take only a dime and when I've lost that to the telephone booth to check if Alice is home yet – she isn't – I take a seat at the bar and Old Arnold slides a dark glass my way. And I bite my fingernails, watching static on the overhead television, imagining tiny sharks in my belly swimming and thrashing about in roiling tides of stomach acid, gnashing at my stomach walls, trying to get out.

I met Alice in college. Or while *she* was in college, rather. I was a young gardener. It did not take long before she wanted always to be around me and I couldn't remember what in Hell I was ever doing before we started dating.

Six feet from approaching her, shuffling through piles of crisp, red and brown leaves out in the courtyard at the university, without turning around she says, happily, surprised, 'Oliver.' She knows my footfalls well, which comforts me in a way I can't explain, especially in that ever since I woke up I'd felt that nobody could see me. It's a dark feeling. But I forget about this, the nearer I get to her.

Her legs are crossed and she is hunched over a small typewriter. I sit down in front of her, crossing my legs and putting my hands on her knees. She is warm through her jeans; momentarily I picture a fire I would've liked to set, anywhere, burning anything. Early on I found that I liked the way her bones feel; they seem to fit inside my every hold on her as if I were a merely a socket; something Alice was specifically designed to connect to. I think of fires again, of electrical fires, of the heat in our bodies and the heat in hers that I want to touch in every way possible. She looks like something out of a nightmare, in a way; something too provocative, too interesting to want to be part of my sullen, effectless life; something I made up. But for the cylinders of Hell I shoved myself through all those times when I couldn't help but to think it, she does want to be a part of my life. It astounds me. I feel grateful, though. In some ways I felt that maybe I meant something after all, truly. It astounds me every moment, her. And in a lot of ways that confuses me, but like always with most things I regularly shrugged it off and tried just not to do anything that would fuck the whole thing up. It was taking the pathway to grace, if grudgingly, feeling blindly along on the way, just letting things happen.

A silent kick to the backside to say to myself 'Just don't.'

Because those who question miracles are a distinctly needy bunch, and far from it, I chose always to let the world happen. To let her world happen to me and make it our world.

Her eyes are closed, lips pursed. It's the kisses that get to me when it's not that silent touch at night, when it's not the way she worms her hands around me like the bones moving under her skin are made of insects. From behind me, I hear somebody screaming but I don't look up. Neither does Alice, whose hair is long and straight and black as dead bodies underground. When she leans in to kiss me without opening her eyes, I close mine and wait for her face to draw closer. I can feel the heat from her lips before we touch, but when our lips do actually meet it doesn't feel as hot as I seemed surely warned of.

When she opens her eyes, they see practically nothing except for a single blank layer that I would at first say is black, but for the fact that she doesn't have a sense of color and so I shouldn't exactly guess what it is her eyes are coming up with in the wake of having nothing to draw upon.

She reaches toward my face, fingers splayed. My eyes draw closed again at the nearness of her hand, until she touches so very lithely the lids of my eyes. 'What have you been doing all morning?' she asks softly, feeling tiny half-revolutions that my eyes are making to benefit her touch.

'Well,' I sigh. Unexcitedly, cynically 'I'm starting to come close to nearing the possible conclusion that perhaps I am maybe beginning to somewhat find a distinct displeasure in the understanding that what may come next in life is certainly just probably a more accurate way of surely deciding that whatever it is that's needing a good look into is absolutely and quite effortlessly and positively *the greatest collection of astoundingly carelessly compiled re-arrangements of tidbits and selections of droll inaccuracies that the world itself has ever, if I should* dare *say, known. Know what I mean?'*

She laughs and all my cares are torn to shreds, turned to confetti. Her voice is a party. A welcome-home celebration.

'I really don't know,' she says, laughing, pulling a cloth over the keys of the typewriter. To myself, I feel better knowing she's going to stop working on her papers to be with me. I snicker at the typewriter, mouth the word Goodbye to it. Half-heartedly, I begin to raise my middle finger toward the typewriter, then feel embarrassed for myself and I stop, but still glare at the keys hidden under the cloth.

'I'm tired of that kind of thing,' I say matter-of-factly but with little seriousness. 'If people can't get through their days without waking up, then what's going to happen in a few years?'

Alice puts her hands on my knees, softly laughing so that only I can hear her.

'Oliver, what the hell does that mean?' she sings.

I have no idea. 'I don't know. Forget about it. Want to go home?'

'Classes,' she concludes, rhythmically apologetic.

'But you always have classes.'

'That's because I'm a student. That's what students do when they're at school. You don't hear me getting bitchy with you when you're busy snipping flowers, do you?'

'Hey, baby. Drop out. Let's drop out of our classes and let's leave this whole city.'

'Oliver, you're not in school.'

'Let's burn this place to the ground.' I am hardly kidding.

'You're hopeless,' she says, smiling, and then kisses me. Sometimes I pretend that darling face of hers is instead fitted with a shark's jaw and that her teeth are several rows of razors from a shark's disgusting mouth. Just a little experiment to try to fool myself into seeing her as ugly for a second or two right before any intimate moment, like kissing or sex. A hammerhead shark, because those look awful. A hammerhead shark's head and shoulders on a decomposing woman's body, plastered over a table at the morgue. A hammerhead's face and an even larger shark's open maw. I would do this because I wanted to see if I still needed to kiss her as badly as I usually did. And always, as it were, the shark thing never worked, because I wanted her so badly I could picture her as just about anything and it would still be attractive. A dead bird. A gutted pig. Some trash outside of a building. Anything. The bulging tongue of a man long hanged but newly discovered. Or the bites carved into his neck from the rope, now green and deteriorated. Alice was that pretty.

I wait at the station for over an hour, unable to recall when her train is due but scared to ask anyone at the ticket booth for fear of having missed its arrival. It had felt like worms in my stomach when I put Alice on that train and sent her home alone, because her mother was dead and the funeral was something I didn't want to be a part of, at all. I'd have driven her there to Pellborough myself, but somehow she'd have ended up coaxing me into staying for the duration of the trip. She was only gone a day when I started to feel like I'd let her down immensely.

Another train comes crawling from the blackness beyond and it nestles itself into the unloading dock under hot white lights. I can't remember what train number she's on, but when the whistle blows and the speakers in the lobby crackle 'Pellborough From St. Bell Isle' my body nearly falls from relief and I collapse down in a bench to catch my breath, an angry, vengeful tension mounting in me, against me.

My fingers feel icy. My feet are encased in cement. I wring my hands and shake my legs out, but it won't break away. I wonder what her family must think of me, after this week.

When I chance a look up, a sharp pang of guilt sticks in my belly and Alice is walking across the platform to the luggage pick-up, skipping behind her antsy seeing-eye dog Pyramids, who is dragging her away from the train, no doubt stifled from the ride.

I'm dreading what she will say to me and I hope her voice is not tinged with hidden disappointment, because I know that if she's angry I put her on a train instead of driving her, that she was left to go through the funeral alone without me, she's not going to tell me as much. She'll hide it and try to forget it. But Alice never forgets anything. Sometimes, I want to trade heads with her so she'll be using my own paltry thought capacity, for then without fail she'll surely forget all that I do or have done that is not heroic. And then when I switch back, we can be on good ground, again. I don't think I have ever really *disappointed* her much before – at least not in any grand way – but something about this one scares me. My head spins. I picture that huge tree, again. It's holding massive arms out for Alice, beckoning, rustling leaves off from the branches, silently suggesting '*Come to me.*' Trying to get her away from me, using as bait all the great things it's done *as a tree*, using this unfair lure by noting all the things I *haven't* done.

For a split second, I find myself cursing that goddamned tree *yet again*, but switch instantly to cursing myself for not being able to get a goddamned tree *out of my thoughts*. It's excruciatingly embarrassing to realize I'm feeling jealous over a tree.

I'm wandering…

If I were to jump in front of one of the slow-moving trains and only hurt myself *a little*, I know she'd put her anger aside. The proposition becomes a definite consideration in my head. Diverting her attention is not entirely below me at this point.

But I still don't even know if she's upset about it yet, so I should just stay calm. I'm hoping maybe the overwhelming sadness of her mother's death will eclipse it, anyway. In fact, that's what I feel like praying for, but I don't want anybody to see me on my knees right now, praying in a train station. Pyramids will come running up to me and he'll start barking. The dog doesn't ever bark, actually, but bad things can happen at anytime.

They don't need a history.

The night before she came back I'd spent the evening at her house, staring dutifully at cobwebs forming in the garage, the spiders making it look like some kind of inhuman lair, thinking to myself that if I'd only try hard enough, for once just *concentrate*, they'd shift forms, turn themselves into butterfly nets and *capture me*, kill me, swallow me, lose me. It was getting warmer by the moment and so still I could feel my skin gathering dust. More dust settled on the old dust, already there.

The film reel image of the subway train windows galloping by in the tunnels blinked in my head, for a little bit. Fast footage of everyone doing nothing but letting time pass. All those people, staring, yawning, or already sleeping as the train pummeled the tracks. It wracked my head. If, in one of the frames, someone had a fat shark's fin stuffed into his or her mouth, pushed against the back wall of the train, with their jaw employed as the handle – their head a weapon, breaking the steel binding over the windows – if that was what happened when the bones in my legs disappeared and I staggered toward a bench behind me to sit, rest and nod off, if that was what happened when I hit a cement beam instead and righted myself, acting as though it never happened. Wobbly, still gazing at spider webs, I dash from the garage, into the house.

I needed to get *out* of the house, though. Being there without Alice was beginning to make me sick. Or afraid. Something I couldn't understand or put a position to. And I wanted desperately to forget whatever it was.

Later, drinking at Pill's, I realize I haven't slept in days. This fact hits me with a supremely horrific chill that I'm sure has left claw marks on my spinal column – if not pushing a few of the discs askance. It also dawns on me that instead of sleeping, replacing the dark hours when my eyes should have been nailed shut, that I'd been in the subway, watching other people doing it – *sleeping* – on benches, or leaning against the passenger windows as trains chugged by, hacking the tracks in a click-click-click click-click-click lullaby. Before the sun would rise, I would find myself at my own place, between the two large hedges outside my apartment, looking over how the last stragglers from the street would pull in after dark, pop a light on somewhere up in the house and then promptly take it away again, fast asleep in a matter of moments while I sipped from a glass of beer in the darkness, watching dust motes settle on the moon, with my head whirling, dizzy from lack of sleep.

Not a single table out of the ten or so at Pill's is occupied. I walk between tables and empty chairs, up to the front.

The bar is sleek and black, lined with polished chrome, all the way down. In the glow of a television set, there are small spatters of cigarette ash and handprint smears. I rest my bare elbows on the chrome, watching my reflection distort in a red glare from the murky overhead lamps.

When I sit down, a small lady hobbles over from where she's been rinsing out glasses. The front of her neck is wrinkled well into her shirt, skin folds concealing more wrinkles in the shadows. 'What'll it be, kiddo?' And just like that, skipping reels, several drinks later my mind blinks like the subway film reel, but there is no color and no people occupy the trains and my body goes from a pained rigidity to being formless as jelly, in seconds, sliding down over the stool. Relief coils around me until I pass out cold.

When I woke, it was at a small table by the wall. Had I been picked up and nestled into a seat? I don't remember. I was passed out.

But the booth I was in now was not unoccupied. Someone else was resting his head in the chair at the other side of the table, passed-out, too, looking to be in the shape I'd just woken from. Actually, sleeping in the same position I was, too. His short, wavy hair had fallen into a mess over his head, haphazardly covering his face. I looked around. There was still nobody at the pool tables. Three people up at the bar, though. The same small old lady, rinsing shot glasses. She didn't look up at me when I stirred. From the looks of the occupants of the table – myself and the other – I deduced maybe this happens here every night.

Fumbling through my pockets for some cash to pay the tab, I scrutinized the young man sleeping in front of me. Something about his coat looked familiar. And his hair. Perhaps I knew him.

Still quite drunk, but reasonably amplified by the mysterious spasm of being jolted from such a sudden catnap, I reached over and gave him a soft pat on the shoulder. For a moment only, his torso expanded with the intake of a heavy breath, soon let out. The breath of his sleep then returned to a quiet pattern. I patted him again, using slightly more force, but he could not be roused from his dozing.

I'd known such slumber myself, once or twice before. Tonight, as a matter of fact. Better to let him wake up on his own or when the barkeep was ready to close the doors and call it a night.

'Have a good one,' I whispered to him.

Rising to get the tab taken care of and also eager to head back to Alice's house to find if I could actually sleep the whole night through again like I hadn't done in days, I took one last glance at the sleeper before parting ways. I couldn't pick out why, but he looked awfully familiar in a very peculiar way, although I could not catch much of his face other than a cheekbone.

The way his arms curled inward and overlapped as he slept was too fucking familiar.

The impression was uncanny, giving me a sharp chill. And for some reason, I couldn't shake the feeling that if he was someone I knew, this would perhaps be something I would not want to know.

The closer she gets, the more I am charged. Grief and longing disappear and all I want to do is touch her, to set all this agitation at ease. To kill it. Her complexion is waxen but bright in a way that means she is thrilled to be with me again – which I am now happier to embrace than I ever thought I could be. At her lithe touch I get the sense that she is teaching me a lesson about sticking by her side, because gradually the hollowness drains from my body with her hands on me. The skin cells on my face and arms instantly begin a rejuvenation process. In the reflection of hers, the settings of my eyes don't look so much like pits.

My body is weak. I can hear the bones in my shoulders creaking under the stress of her touch. My chest and lungs, filled with good, pure air, scented as lavender from her hair, they surge, and my knuckles seem to gain color as well as the power to hold her as tight as I should.

With tears threatening to pour, I look into her soft green eyes, at a small circle of blackness in her pupil, at my reflection, and I think to myself *Inside there . . . is where I want to stay from now on.*

An eternity passes in seconds, galloping along subway tracks, blinking past me in dark tunnels. The drive home is a blur. I am surprised at myself, but not surprised at all. I don't really even know myself, nor do I really want to. Everything seems fine now that Alice is home again. Before I know it, we are kissing against the kitchen sink, her hands at my hips while I steady our balance with my elbows propped across the counter tops.

I try to picture a fat gray walrus at the zoo, sucking down on the head of some hyperactive child who has hopped the rail, while his hands scrape madly at the creature's face, trying with grand, endearing futility to get away. His flushed little hands scrape at the fat gray rubbery face, pulling at the tusks until he is neck-deep in its mouth, slumping down lifelessly after a sharp crack of the neck. The back of his shirt is soaking red against the last few death spasms that ignite and then suddenly flare out.

Alice's skin is so soft. I expect to find a pair of angel's wings pushing from her back when I pull her shirt off, but she is only soft and smooth, with small bumps in her spine protruding from the skin, and I run my fingers up along her back and down again.

Later, when we are both watching the moonlight trace shadows around tree branches across the ceiling, it is warm in her bed. And when her touch fades, I know she has fallen into sleep. Gradually, my lids become heavy and it feels astoundingly new and perfect. My body is warm with a sense of peace and the fingers I run along her smooth arm start to lose direction, the power to guide them losing substance as I follow her into sleep.

That was the last nap I had for four days. It would also be the last wedge of sleep I would know in twice as many.

A pair of hedge clippers trail off excitedly in a direction I did not push them. With two fingers nicked, thick washes of blood paint my hand and the clippers take a while to rip through my pants and saw a trench into my leg. The blood feels more profuse than it really is and I am able to drive to the hospital and walk out an hour later, with spider webs of stitches in my hand and leg. I decide to take the rest of the day off.

The doctor said my eyes were too round and weary, that I should get some sleep. He prescribed some pills to help me achieve this. I don't know where the insomnia came from and at first I didn't even know that's what it was. I figured I was just getting sick, that my body was too hot, that my blood pressure was boiling, that my body sought to – temporarily – betray me. Or that I missed Alice so much. Or that I was worried about how she felt about the death of her mother. Or that she was hurt I didn't want to pay my last respects to the dead woman. Or that she was hurt because I wasn't by her side during such a tragic moment in her life. Or that I let her down. Or that I was getting sick.

But during the second night, dead tired, I realized I had almost no real thoughts in my head. Everything was mushy, like marrow. No faction of subject matter stayed in my head for more than three seconds. Empty, feeling hollow, I tossed myself around to every corner of the bed, rolled myself into a host of promising positions but could find no comfortable purchase. I lay there prone, solid cement with fixed eyes staring at the ceiling, wearily attempting to blink as the tiles began fuzzily changing shape.

The darkness played tricks with my eyes, but it could not and would not push me asleep.

So I got up and went for a drive into the city, where I parked my car before an expired meter and crawled into the hot earth to ride the subway underneath town for hours and hours.

When other train cars passed the one I was in, going in the opposite direction, I could see very fragmented scenes cutting up and splicing themselves together in the disproportionate film reel that I've come to recognize as a metaphor for how I am living my life. And then it seemed there was a plot to all this that wouldn't be hard for me to grasp if I could only sit up and pay enough attention. In the green neon of the train cars, stale-looking people stood with the hoods of their sweatshirts pulled up over their eyes. Some of them were gazing at nothing, resigned and tired. A few of them – most of them – were chatting with other passengers. Tired, rubbing their eyes for want of sleep.

Some of them had their heads against the glass, already dreaming.

When I got back home, the sun was almost up. The world was getting light blue. I wasn't necessarily tired anymore, but very weak.

Alice calls to tell me she loves me, and that feels good. My head swirls. I despair to think of her at the office, doing something important, drafting plans she can't even *see* while I have the whole world at the edge of my eyes and I have yet to see a real goddamned solution to anything my entire life.

Then it occurs to me, like a rock to the face, that while I don't necessarily care so much about me, that although it seems I have no ambition in life and no direction, this is not entirely true. For Alice *is* my ambition, it now seems. And she's my *direction*. To be with her is my only real goal in life.

The thought feels too easy. But I can't find a way to prove it wrong.

Marveling at this, feeling proud that I really *do have* a goal in life after all, that I want to do something great and I am working for it all the time without even knowing it, simply by wanting to be with her and for her to be happy, I crash against the side of the tree. Chips of bark rain down on me. I catch some of them and throw them into the eyes of a couple of squirrels standing about, nibbling on acorns. My newfound ambition is a heavy feeling and for it I feel the express need to sit.

Squirrels scatter as I take a few steps forward into this new life.

There's a thin walkway between a thick rise of bushes to either side, mounted behind two tiny benches that stare at each other like mirrors. Lowering myself into one of them, sliding down so that my shoulders are practically supporting me against the back of the bench, I cross my legs and bury my hands in my jacket.

And – miraculously – I nod off.

Peacefully. I actually sleep.

Thunder grumbles calmly in the sky, almost cooing the clouds. Behind my eyes I can see those clouds, gently sliding across the sky, black and gray but not menacing. Thunder hushes the bustling little city and people start to pack their things and head for cover, warned.

Smiling, in a dream of even calmer floods soothingly washing over a crowded town square as heads disappear in the murk, random hands grasping at the sultry air above the black spiraling floodwater, I am suddenly jolted awake.

Alarmed at the abruptness of springing up, but instantly calmed for such an invigorating and sudden nap, I smile at the first light sprinkling droplets of soft rain, letting the gentility of it cool on my face. I sit there with my hands in my jacket pockets, relaxed. Who'd have thought sleep should come to me so effortlessly? And here, on a walk, of all places. I am feeling good. Really ready to go out there and not let the whole world seem so crowded and ruthless. I am going to walk to a flower peddler on the street in the park and I'll buy the largest bouquet of the sweetest smelling flowers he's willing to let go of and I'll tip him what's left of my money and I'll walk the flower bouquet to Alice's office myself and place them on the table because she loves the smell of fresh flowers and...

This is when I see the person on the other side of the thin walkway, opposite me. He is slumped down into the bench opposite mine, still sleeping even as the rain picks up. The sounds of traffic and rainfall around me are rough against each other, like stones slowly scraping together.

I stand, jarred. With his legs crossed and his hands cuddled into the pockets of his jacket, a sweep of hair covering his downcast face, I recognize him *instantly*.

It's the same guy from the bar that I'd woken to find sleeping across from me at the small booth the night before Alice came back.

It seems absurd. But, yes. It's the very same man.

A small attempt to get closer to him stops me dead in my tracks, as I realize that not only is it the same guy, but he's dressed in the same clothes that I am.

Not completely without reason, I am paralyzed. All except for my head and neck, which I crane from side to side in an attempt to situate myself, gazing in every direction possible to make sure I am really here. The park is empty. The rain grows insistent.

It becomes a downpour, but the man sleeping before me is not stirring. His chest rises and falls rhythmically, pushing his chin up in short feats of movement. That short-cropped wavy hair – uncombed yet not threatening to become a mess – that is a very *familiar* haircut. It is one I seem to know very well, as if I see it every day.

The rain is now pouring so hard that I am forced to make a choice. Either I stand here and stare at this . . . stranger, or I make a break for it and get out of the cold before I become sick.

'Hey man,' I shout. 'It's raining. You'd better get up.'

There is no response. The sleeper is unprovoked from his slumber. He moves not a muscle, except for the slow and steady rising of the chest with intake of air. It is when I start to give another shout that the full comprehension that he is wearing the same brown slacks and pale yellow button-down that I too am wearing hits me. Hard. That he is being kept moderately warm, if not entirely dry, by the same kind of coat that I am wearing. Not merely this, but that his pants are not simply the same *design* as the clothes on me, but the very same shirt and pants and jacket, too. Right down to worn patches and loose threads. It is when I realize this person is a replica of me that I run.

And the park becomes a fading yet doggedly insistent memory at Pill's, where I pound two shots of bourbon before buying a round for Old Arnold – who declines. Downing his refused shot myself and then buying a round each for two strangers staring glumly into empty glasses on either side of me, I lose track of the beers I am drinking. Easily. It becomes round after steady round after round.

When I arrive later at Alice's office, waiting for her in the lobby, it is awful to realize that I am unerringly, *gravely* sober.

My body feels like an empty shell when she scoots directly toward me across the carpet in the lobby, feeling me there, knowing exactly where I am. She can feel my presence and though this should – and would, regularly – come as a resounding comfort, instead her embrace seems to make me flinch. Though I am, by now, quite dry, she says 'Christ, Oliver, you're *shivering*.' She touches my neck with her lips. 'Oh my God, you're *freezing*, baby.'

I want to sprawl out across the backseat of the car, or at the least just huddle into the passenger seat and cower as she drives. But I'm always the designated driver – naturally – and while she sits comfortably beside me, gently squeezing my knee, I fight hard to act normal. And though what I would really like to do right now is pull over to the side of the road and go running off into the woods to disappear, I smile at her. She can't see me, but I get the sense she knows I am smiling at her anyway. And yes, she *smiles right back at me*, leans forward and kisses my neck. 'You're still so cold, Oliver. Are you okay?'

My hands are trembling and I can actually feel the stitches in my leg worming around like a pile of ants in and out of my skin and I'm not even *half* okay, which makes me even *more* nervous, knowing that I *should* feel okay with Alice here. I try to picture the lines of cars parked at the sides of the road as beached whales baking in the sun, but when it changes nothing, I realize there's no reason at all to be doing this. But it's no good. I keep driving past shiny, chrome and steel beached whales that do nothing but serve to freeze me yet more and I can't stop pretending because I want this all to be made instantly better.

I can't for the life of me make any sense out of procedure at this point and I race through a few red lights, which despite the situation being as eerie as it truly is still makes me feel bad, since I'm supposed to be the responsible one here in the car. Pyramids is in the backseat, eyeing me, seeing what Alice thankfully cannot. And though he's not growling at me, for the first time I wish he would. It's just too quiet in the car.

'Yeah, baby. I'm…' I struggle to complete the sentence, but I'm too cold. I'm too fucking tired to make sense. 'Fine,' I finish, sucking in a deep breath.

I didn't find sleep during the night. The approach of a spider or cockroach crawling across the bed in the moonlight would have been a welcome discomfort, but Alice's house is always kept immaculately clean. Tonight it seems the house is hollow, with nobody in it and nothing else. I am unable to hold her when Alice holds me. I am still an empty shell and I'm thinking about the other body. Not the beautiful one purring next to me, but that other sleeping one at the park.

Worry washes over me so profoundly I sweat myself into a small pool on the bed. Thankfully, she is asleep. I can't get it out of my head, turning over what was possibly in Alice's thoughts right now. I kick myself a thousand times, trying to get to sleep.

But it will be days before I can do so.

I'm supremely thankful Alice cannot physically see what I look like, because I think I must resemble a proper bag of bones. A weary hitchhiker. A ghost haunted by other ghosts. She touches my eyes in the morning and asks me if I have slept okay. I tell her fine. She doesn't believe me, but I sound confident about it – which surprises me – so instead of lying it probably just sounds like I had a nightmare and chose not to babble on about it. She makes breakfast and I read the ingredients on a box of pancakes, thinking it sounds like a recipe for making quicksand. I picture slipping through the sand, with one hand left clutching empty air. Breakfast feels silly. I try to shrug off yesterday. Remarkably, it half-way works. And by the time I'm out under the fan of a shade tree, pushing heaps of mulch around a bed of gorgeous green lilies, I smile. The effort it takes to do so is not lost on me, but I continue, thinking, deeply wishing that Alice could see this. I wish she could see me do this. It may be a worthless little flowerbed, but it's a small fragment of the world that I somehow managed to make attractive and I suddenly wanted and desperately needed her to see I was capable of doing this.

Sharp is the knife of regret that cuts through me when I am humiliated here in the garden, alone, by the thought of Alice gazing down at these flowers. Who am I kidding?

Of all that she could use her eyes on if she *were* to suddenly, magically gain sight, to think this shitty little nest of green flowers should mean much? I cannot decide whether this is selfishness or mere nit-picking, but it's obviously a black cloud.

Lunch becomes half of a half-sandwich, washed down with snowstorm-cold glasses of beer. In the heated bar, the ice that falls down my throat sort of freezes my mind.

I push out all recollection of the garden. Gone too are the grumpy barflies and the buzzing of traffic, filtering in from outside. I allow myself to grow numb to all feeling and without knowing it, the pain and nervousness and the humiliation all disappear. From a booth in the corner, I hail the bartender and have two more drinks set before me. But before I can guzzle down even half of one, the comfort I feel is so miraculous that, while still sober – however impossible that should seem – my forehead nuzzles the warm oak finish of the table and I simply . . . pass . . . out.

Two glasses of beer fly through the air and crash down on the floor beside the table. The terrible, guilt-drenched sound it makes is deafening, yet nothing is stirring in the bar. It was as if a pin had been pulled from me and I exploded like a bomb.

How it's possible to smash glasses in a quiet little bar and still sit here without attracting attention is beyond me, but whimpering like a dog, panting in fast, helpless gasps, I wish to trade the entire world for just a little company. *Anybody. Somebody* to come over here and see this. But *nobody* is looking in my direction. And so nobody is seeing what I am seeing, at this booth.

What made me panic when I woke was that I was not alone in the booth upon waking.

Sitting across from me, positioned exactly how I was, with his head back just a little, just like me, though with his face somewhat hidden behind the shoulder, was *me*.

There was no mistaking it. Dressed exactly as I was. But even if he weren't wearing my clothes too, it was *still me*, beyond any form of doubt. The man sleeping across from me was a mirror image, mimicking in his slumber every last concrete detail accurately, incontrovertibly particular to me. Even the stubble on his face, how it was thicker at the chin and under the nose.

Nearly falling over myself, I somehow carry my body to the bar and speaking now like I'm crazy, I openly suggest the bartender have a look at the smashed glasses and the spilled mess at the booth. Pulling to the side to gain a better view, he glances over my shoulder at the broken glass and the beer soaking into the booth and into the floorboards, then back at me, curiously, visually disappointed but obviously not surprised. He says to me tiredly 'Better call it a day, pal. That'll be ten bucks.'

I lean in toward him. 'Don't you think you ought to have a look at the booth, though?'

Squinting at me, he leans back as much as I've leaned forward, unsure of what I am getting at. 'For . . . what?'

'Maybe there's something in the *booth* you ought to *see*?'

The second he puts his two hands on the bar and leans into me, staring hard, no longer mystified or curious but now teeming with anger, I realize this is going to end right now and I'm going to pay my tab and never come to this bar again. Walking faster and faster toward the door, I chance a look back over my shoulder and the bartender is still glaring at me. My flight is halted when I hit the side of my face against the doorjamb and the handle digs into my stomach. With an exaggerated cry of alarm, I turn toward the bartender again, who looks like he's ready to make a move if I don't leave.

The last thing before I am out on the street again is the bartender grumbling, still with hands on the bar, to no one in particular 'Goddamned asshole drunks.'

But the thing is, I'm not drunk. Sure, I want to be. But I'm not.

I'm not even *near* drunk. What I am is *tired*. That catnap was nothing. And how the hell am I expected to sleep much, anyway? I mean, look at this. Look at what's happening.

I could find another bar easy. A dark one with tiny, shadowed booths. But, no. That's obviously a bad idea. *But*, I can find a dark, lowly little place too small for privacy or even booths and I can sit *at* the bar and I can stay there until Alice gets off work and I can call a cab for her and meet her at her place and tell her I was experiencing problems with the car and that would be that and we would have dinner and maybe watch a movie and then we'd go to sleep – *I would toss and turn while she dreamt*, sure, but I'd be safe with her. And who knows? Maybe I just might actually really fall asleep, tonight. And I'd stay that way until the sun crawled up. I am certainly tired enough to do just that. I need only to relax my body and let it happen. Alice, if nothing else in the world, can do that for me. She'll cuddle up against me with her soft body filling the void between me and the icy air and I would be gently rocked into sleep by her breath. Her chestfalls would lull me.

I walk the whole way to her place and call a cab from the telephone in her kitchen, hand over the fraudulent story of the dysfunction in the car, we have dinner on the couch while watching television, I stare at the screen, I speak but don't hear a word I am saying, she whispers in my ear and laughs but I don't hear a word she is saying. I feel scared. A warning seems to try penetrating me, but I am too numb to accept it. We slip into bed and our hands map each other out and at the back of my head I am being told that the small, creeping feeling I'm trying desperately to grasp is pleasure – or possibly safety. But it may really be dread, because I'm not sure if I am lying to myself or not. But Alice falls to my side and it feels too quick and I know something odd has happened and she turns the light out and the way she nestles against me is something like a search for a comfortable position that is not personal and she is sleeping before the clock hits the top of the hour and I watch, horrified, as the top of the hour turns into the next and one more later, until it is midnight. With a fully developed unease, I turn my head away from the clock while it climbs two more hours, then three. And I am staring at the closet doors in the dark, until slowly the outlines of the wood paneling become clearer as the sun begins to rise, the slats on the doors moving fuzzily as I stare helplessly at their repetitions. And at six-thirty, her alarm sounds. I snap it off before she is roused and wake her manually.

This scenario happens for a couple more days, until I start turning her alarm off almost as soon as she's nodded off. And unable to take my eyes from the clock for too long at any one moment during the night, I spend the entire night in bed regarding the numbers on the clock as tiny monsters. I wake her up on my own, by pushing lightly against her shoulder and saying her name.

She takes these actions a different way, however, finding it sweet that I should rise before her just to wake her up. Like this is all purposeful.

God bless her.

How sweet it is that she should not know what dreadfulness I hold from her during the night. How dark the sunlight looks when it becomes apparent that distinguishing between night and day is, stressingly, maddeningly, simply not necessary anymore.

Deciding once again to call it quits for the day – even though I still have more than a few yards left to address before the weekend is over – I'd clapped my hands together and brushed the dirt off hours ago, as if a job well done had been completed. Exceedingly far from the truth, as I've truly been *really* shitty about my job lately.

But I feel like black clouds are roaming at the dome of my skull. I sit at a bench outside a smallish diner near the train station and doggedly, completely focused, I watch the front doors for a few hours.

When the only people to come out of the building for a long while happen to be other people and not anyone that looks exactly like me, I grow antsy and tired. And not wanting to accidentally fall asleep again, I get up and stretch. That this should not be happening, right now. I *should* still be at work, planting yellow roses. This is not lost on me. And the embarrassment is only held in check by the humility and the paranoia that follows it. Robotically – every move punched in on the machine I am now – I cross the street through a minor snow flurry and slowly enter the diner, making my way sluggishly toward the back with a determination that I feel might be a little premature, though I'm absolutely unable to help it. And I walk steadily toward the corner table – where I'd sat earlier in the day and passed out – to see if the sleeping body that appeared upon waking is still there. Or if it's at least awake, now.

Chills encompass me and I actually shiver there in the corner of the diner, even though it's not at all cold, because hunched in the table, in the precise position he was in when I last saw him, is me. Sleeping. Another me.

It's a replica of me, fast asleep at that table. Down to the same fucking shoelaces. But *it's not me*. It can't fucking be me. I cover my mouth to stifle a scream, momentarily impressed that I'm even this composed, considering what's going on. I'm nearly paralyzed with dread, but then an altogether separate energy in me propels me toward the sleeper and I shove him, hard. 'Get up,' I say, loudly.

But the figure does not stir. He sleeps on, unmoved.

I shove him, again. Then again, even harder. 'Get up,' I plead, forcefully. But he does nothing. Still scared, still feeling like I'm crazy, but unable to turn around to see if somebody is staring at me, I first punch him in the back of the head and then push him right out of the seat and his body falls heavily to the floor, with his head propped up against the wall. I gasp, because this is the first time I've seen its whole face – his face – and that face is mine. There is no longer any seed of doubt and the worry and horror becomes titanic. So I start kicking mercilessly at the body, screaming 'Get up! Get Up!'

Hands are now pulling at me. There are angry voices spitting in my ear. And I am being pulled from the table. A fist is hailed repeatedly at my face, with a warning for me to stop or he – the speaker – would break my whole face. But I keep kicking that unwaking version of me who is slumped down against the wall under all of the commotion.

'Get off him, man!' somebody shouts. 'Leave him alone!' another.

'Get him out of here!' somebody else adds.

'But fucking *look* at him!' I scream, screeching 'Let me go!' Wild, now. Flailing. 'It's me! It's me!'

A fist is sunk into my stomach, the powerful blow effectively silencing me. Falling back, I reach to grasp out for a chair or anything to balance myself, but hit the wall and lose all certainty of balance. Somebody's shouting, but the words are all accusatory and thankfully I am too distracted to understand what it means. I still pull a little, trying for release, but it is no good. And I am dragged from the diner and pushed out onto the sidewalk. People are staring at me with expressions ranging from horrified to amused. It's exactly what I pictured happening, all the other times when I was afraid to point attention to the fucking *twin* sleeping its soundless, ghostly sleep next to me. There's some fat, frazzled cook standing above me in a white undershirt that's draped with a stained white smock, waving his thick spatula at me and kicking me, too. The spatula is one of those heavy steel models that does not bend and he swings it deeply through my face, slicing the cheek open while it spits grease at me and he's screeching, all the while. I don't understand what he's saying. But somebody else kicks me in the ribs to back him up on it, saying if I don't leave I'll be pulverized. I am kicked a few more times. I no longer understand anything in my life.

Tears are filling my eyes up like clogged drains and everyone who is yelling at me starts to shimmer and swim around. When somebody kicks me in the face the water is emptied from my sockets and I see everyone fine again, but the tears keep coming and soon they are all drowned and shimmering, and I'm glad I can't see this.

How can nobody have witnessed what really happened? Didn't anyone notice how I pushed that guy against the wall and he *still* did not rise from sleep? Or that, worse still, he was dressed the same as I was? And that his face was my mirror image? Didn't anyone see that?

Do people normally get knocked around like that in this restaurant without waking up to defend themselves? Jesus, they *can't* have seen him. Maybe it was a ghost.

But I'm not dead. It can't be a ghost.

If all of this is in my head, then I have to keep this from Alice, at all costs. She can never know that I am seeing these things, or else it is the end of us. But this is really happening. Who else can I go to but her?

This whole situation could mean that something more awful still is about to happen and that these horrific events are just mediocre premonitions of something even worse. But who could I possibly confide in but Alice? And how could I possibly explain this to her?

Rubbing my eyes, limping, I head for the subway, hoping the noise of trains will distract me.

It doesn't. But I still feel better here, where there are lots of people all around me. I haven't been to a bar in weeks, thinking the fragmentation of mind or the hallucination of waking up to find myself beside myself, *sleeping*, may actually be alcohol related. But it's not. No matter how much I try to drink – as an experiment – I cannot help but to remain morbidly sober. And yet those *things* appear whenever I am pulled from the few sudden, restless bits of sleep my body is awarded with. And what a fucking reward it is, after all. My body is wracked from exhaustion and every effort I take to appear like a regular human being when I'm around Alice feels to me as forced as a high school play. She must surely know that all is not well. But yet she keeps this from me. She may not be able to see, but Christ, she must *see* this is happening *somehow*.

On the train, shooting through tunnels under the city, the cars are very dimly lit, and my bones hurt from lack of sleep and also a discomforting malnutrition I've been nursing since I stopped drinking and stopped feeling like I have my head screwed on right.

Whatever is happening to me is well beyond my capacity to understand. And it's been occurring enough for me to not fully find myself so much surprised as shocked and steadfastly, unspeakably horrified. My throat tightens and to utter a single word seems an impossibility. The steady click-click-click click-click-click underneath the subway train, surrounding me on all sides, envelopes me and I tap my fingers against the inside of the window as limitless darkness unfolds between well-spaced haunches of fluorescent-lit cement and crowds of sleepy travelers hustling to and from work, to and from homes. And I don't feel like I have a home, anymore. Since I can't fall asleep like a regular person, my apartment has become haunted. The bed looks and acts like a monster. When I touch the mirror, it is icy against my fingertips, fogging up. When I call Alice from the telephone, her answering machine picks up and that constant message – *I'll get back to you, as soon as I can* – now is a direct threat to me.

Or a curse. And yes, maybe a warning too. Maybe everything is a warning, now.

Being a target is easy for relatively few, so I take what solace I can in that and don't feel too bad about how I'm handling this so far, remembering that erosion is something that takes time to occur, and I compose myself – if fraudulently – like a half-real human being.

The picture painted on my face is that of absolute normalcy. Despite the black, swollen pits of my eyes, the gaunt cheeks jutting out at the bone like distended icebergs, and my lips being sore and chapped from licking them nervously, I think I'm doing rather well acting as if none of this is inherently wrong. Just to get through the day.

I mean, I can still go through the motions of preparing a salad at the cafeteria salad bar under the offices Alice works in, and the looks I get seem to reflect that I'm acting right, like a real person, and when I put coins into the telephone booth, my hands don't shake like I'm a drug addict.

So I'm getting along fine, I think. At least as far as other people are concerned. I have to go back to work sooner or later, or I will lose all of my gardening accounts. I have to find my way back to something.

There is something I must reclaim, this much is true. What that is, I'm not sure. But I've been stolen from. Some kind of regularity has been ripped from me that I can't understand. Some kind of human right has been denied me. Perhaps the right to understand day and night? The right to a dreamless sleep? The right to any amount of safe sleep?

I want to stop calling her place, especially as I can no longer distinguish what time of the day I am placing these calls. It's not that I can't read a clock, but that the numbers themselves are conscious now, breathing individually of their own will. And they lie to me. Time passes by so slow, that when it's three in the morning I think the clock must surely be broken, it can't possibly be that late. If one were to consciously study my actions, in some drugstore or a library or a fast food restaurant, perhaps it would appear to the average person that I have fallen into a state of heavy drug use. Maybe it's starting to tell on me, after all. To me I look sick, I act sick, I make no sense and can make sense of nothing. *It's possibly the lack of sleep*, I tell myself and so swallow a cupped palm of sleeping pills. But they do nothing for me except to swell in my stomach and swim uselessly there, floating and floating and floating. Growing fat as maggots.

Then I remember it's not the lack of sleep. It's the fact that I'm possibly out of my fucking mind. I have to do something. And it needs to be done right now.

Still tapping the window on the subway train, I pound a fist into my knee, but feel nothing. Pulling a wedge of skin between my index finger and thumb, I pinch it so hard the skin splits and a small spurt of blood shoots across my pant leg, but I can't feel that either. My head is spinning. I'm so sad about all of this that I lean back and I am fucking *defeated*. But this does not stick into me so much, because for it, I actually realize that I am falling asleep.

It's coming in languidly, seeping through my shoulders and riding my arms down to the elbows, loosening my fists. It feels like rest is happening. Giving up, giving in. Is it finally giving me a chance to sleep? It is. I'm nodding off. But I don't feel like this is foreboding. Actually, it feels like I could sit here for another week like this. It's better than it ever has been, this sense of rest. Sitting still, alone in the small row of seats, I let everything go and lean my face against the window and my muscles feel relaxed for the first time in I can't even begin to think how long, now.

My mind is worn-out from being knocked back and forth between knowing what is happening and trying to act like I know. And I am falling asleep.

Consenting and committing to defeat, sleep overtakes me. It climbs my body from below, too.

Yes, the lids are heavy and my entire frame feels rested. Numb, certainly. And weak, without a doubt. But actually *tired* too. Tired, with the effect that exhaustion *should* carry, in that I am nodding off into sleep. A proper sleep. Something I have not known since . . . half a year ago.

Pushing out any further thought of investigation, I simply let it take me.

Jesus Christ, it feels amazing. Already my arms are weightless, becoming thin spirits, light as air. My lungs drag breath in of their own accord without my trying at all and my chest is squeezed into a rhythm, so relaxed, soft waterfalls carrying the breath back out, and rhythmically it repeats while I sit there, doing nothing but *feeling* it.

My eyes have no want, no desire. There is no reason to open my eyes. The tracks are clicking underneath the train, echoing inside the train car, and I can't fucking believe it but *I am falling asleep.*

...as with most all dreams, I do not know how long I have been living this life, but after a long stretch of hopping gracefully over titan buildings of cold, cracked stone, mid-air, swooping down over what looks to me like some kind of a prison, yielding some fantastically shimmering lake carved into the rooftop, I am *conscious* of the dream I am having yet not conscious of what I've been taken from to be here. I only know that this feels like the first dream I have ever known. And it's perfect. My body continues to move slowly, taking hard, determined steps as I run, admitting flight when my legs are ready to push the earth away, again. I am not a giant, I am just unstoppable. I clear entire fields of buildings with one jump. So very fucking easily. Over another building. In this dream, I am simply running...

...there is no destination at all, just some ever forward march. Nothing stands in my way. Not buildings. Not trees. It's beautiful. The winds up in the sky rock me gently in pillowy arms, whisking me softly along as I sail. Upon closer inspection, every structure I leap over, in contrast to the unshackled life flowing through my arms and legs, is a prison, forcing a distinction between the comfort and the very freedom of what I am doing and what it is I'm doing this over. Me, I've been set free. And I'm clearing them one by one, these cement houses, on my way to someplace better. One after the other, all of these buildings are supporting atop their roofs the burden of large, natural bodies of water. Some of the prisons are inscribed with lakes while others host rivers. I continue to run, negligent of time, unable to comprehend fear. The world darts past me and way up in the sky, leaping, free, I laugh at it. On the ground, my steps are ten feet apart. The speed attained outdistances light. The amount of time I spend on the ground is wistfully debatable. It's just *seconds*. I could spit at the thought and my saliva would stretch for hundreds of miles as it splashed. It's useless to measure the time between clearing miles and waiting to hit the sky again. Around the universe in half a wink. The prisons pass under me like pitiable ants. For ages this seems to be, until at last the landscape up ahead shows me a hard fact. It's a promise. What lies ahead of me is incontrovertible. It is…

…because ahead of me there is a large, dark green wall. It stretches higher than I am able to see. It climbs into clouds with one vastly flat, valiant grasp, sneering for its entire length across the horizon in either direction. Gathering strength and speed, my stride does not waver as I pitch through the world, leaping that which would seek to bind me, its lakes and rivers below mere twinkles to my eye as I continue racing toward the wall. Leaping prisons. Leaping entire forests. The wall, however, does not appear to get closer. Still conscious of my dream, my courage is nonetheless threatened, and my surety is now just a mask that I'm using to bluff the dream as I pitch forward…

…nothing matters. I scale entire prisons. Entire countries. Hours pass by like minutes. The wall only appears really *close*, finally, when I am so proximate that I cannot possibly stop in time to avoid collision. But I'm not going to avoid anything. I am here to clear the wall. Because there is no boundary for me, anymore. And nothing to hold me back. The profound reality of shoving my body over fortresses is practically written before me in cloudlike-typed letters and I will not let barriers loom over me anymore. And I push hard on my legs and I dive into the sky…

…the wall I am unable to clear…

…my body smashes into the vast green wall with a devastating clap. The stone is cool and soft, yet hard enough to stop me from cracking it. I do not bounce, but fall straight down. The plummet, the distance, is immeasurable. The ground is worlds away. I know that when I hit the ground, I will wake up…

When I wake up, it's instantly the worst day of my life. There are *two* adaptations sleeping in the seats across from me. There are two. And they are both slumped – fast asleep – in the exact same position I am.

At breakfast, I wash my face with dish soap in the kitchen sink while Alice prepares a pan over the stove. She hums softly to herself as I rinse repeatedly yet don't seem to get the silky dish soap out of my eyes. Temporarily blinded, I reach for a dry dish rag and cut my hand on a knife on the sink. The thought that Alice would never have done this does not escape me. Miraculously, I don't make a sound, instead shoving my whole head under the tap and scrubbing my eyelids until the soap is gone, then I wipe my face dry with the bottom of my t-shirt.

Barely a word is spoken while we eat. I'm poking at the food with a knife, slicing it into ribbons.

'How have you been, lately?' she asks me, her tone loaded with an icy concern I've learned to weed out from the standard gentility. So I don't answer. It's not because I don't have an answer, but that I can't give her this particular answer. And if I try to hide it by contriving an excuse, or even trying to push the real problem aside. She'll know anyway that something is entirely wrong. It's fucking irritating to realize a blind person sees me better than even I do.

It's obvious that because I choose not to answer, she picks her plate up, carries it to the sink, cleans it and the pans and everything else she used to prepare breakfast, then silently disappears from the room. My pancakes look like slashes of thorns and barbed wire to me. If I take another bite, my mouth will be shredded.

My heart sinks when Alice leaves the room, but I am powerless to stop her. I am handicapped. This irony, too, is not lost on me. I feel like taking a nap. The fact that I can't is *also* not lost on me.

What is really lost, as it happens, is me.

It also dawns on me that, well, what would really be gained if I am found?

Half a couple dozen or more – I don't know – telephone messages are blinking at me from the screen on the machine. The number of messages is blinking in double digits, but the numbers just look to me like the thousands of clocks I've stared helplessly, ravenously at for the past month or so. It's just a bunch of red, bloody numbers. After so long – and I'm sure I have been standing here for almost an hour – I reach forward to press *PLAY*.

That's when the power cuts off.

I haven't paid the bill, so it's only natural.

Back under the city, train cars shoot past, round and sleek like water snakes. It breathes in windowed bubbles of sleeping heads, dotting the scales, the windows. When I fall back into a bench, I am heavier than my muscles can best and rather than sigh, I actually crumble.

Jolted from a deep dark sleep that is – thankfully – dreamless, the bench is full, and my arms are crowded, pinned down at my sides. The bench is not merely occupied by others, it's literally packed, so that I am shoulder to shoulder. Gradually, I can muster the power to turn my head. To the right, with just enough room to support someone else, it's me, asleep with his arms pinned at the sides. Swiveling my head to the left, on this tiny bench there are four more semblances of myself, crouched and huddled and wedged on the bench, fast, faithfully asleep. They're *all* me. My head rolls back in maddened horror and I push myself forward. With great effort, I am able to free myself from the packed bench and shoot like a rocket, flailing around as I fall to the cement. People are staring at me. Others waiting for the bus are stepping away.

Pressing my palms against the cold cement, I turn to the cursed bench behind me while attempting to raise myself up again. And there on the bench, with just a small bit of space at the far right where I'd vaulted from, there are five sleeping Olivers.

The next train squeals to a halt. Helplessly, I spring from the ground and into the car. Nobody else on the platform follows, though I know this is the train they've been waiting for. They all just stare, mystified or full of pity as they choose not to get involved. I point across the platform toward the bench I'd just sprung from, screaming 'Look at *them,* you fucking idiots! Not *me!*' pointing wildly toward the haunting row of dozing replicas.

A tiny lady hugs two miniscule children close to her, mouth open in disgust, watching me.

'What the fuck is wrong with you people! *Look at that fucking bench! Don't you see them!*'

Some of the onlookers, indeed, finally turn to look at the bench, but the train's doors slide shut in my face before anyone can turn back to me to confirm anything, eclipsing whatever it was somebody might have said in return upon glancing at the bench. And the train pushes slowly at first, then shoots forward into the dark tunnels.

I wake up again, collapsed against the doors. When I push myself off, there are so many versions of me pushed against the wall of the train, all facing to the right – how I awoke – all of them breathing in and out in unison, that I can no longer stifle what cries I have left to offer. My lungs become hideouts for restless shrieks all coming out of hiding. I become a wailing siren. The duplicates' sighs are so collectively loud that I press my hands over my ears and fight to drown them out with my own screaming.

Bracing myself, I shove the Oliver closest to me and he falls easily, collapsing against the second, toppling the third, who rattles but barely moves the fourth, who is leaning against the wall with a section of seats between him and the third, but he slides slowly against the fifth, who pushes forward and thuds against – resting against – the sixth.

The doors echo as I pound them, desperate to escape. I kick at the sleeping Olivers. Howl at them and punch wildly. Then I turn back to the doors, still wailing. For a moment or two, I actually claw at them, crazed, inevitably *biting* the plastic edges of the wall, attempting at all cost to gnaw my way off this train.

Slowly but surely, the train begins to slow. There is an entire crowd of people at the next stop, which I plan to plunge into. But something in me rages, forcibly calming me, speaking matter-of-factly 'Slow down. Wait. Wait for the doors to open. You cannot do it by strength. You must wait.'

So I step back, composing myself. My body is shaking violently. I fix my shirt, tucking it in, smoothing out the collar, running tense fingers through my hair to smooth it out, too. Walking backwards, I hit the bench behind me and fall into it, facing the doors that are about to open. Watching the grim faces of the perpetually tired outside the doors, I yawn. Forcing back the yawn, I slap myself in the face, something which a few of the people outside the now settled train notice. When the doors open, a few of them – naturally – scrutinize my behavior shrewdly and warily, but regardless, they clamor in, eager to make this train. Their sheer tidal mass is too much and I push back into the bench, shoving my eyes closed, flinching.

I wake up.

Literally drowned in people. Some of them are strangers, but more than half of them are, of course, *me*.

But luckily, when I wake again after having passed out a third or *fourth* time, it's when the train has come to another stop. And absolutely no time is wasted shoving directly through the crowd, blindly, whoever the fuck they are, bundles of me or bunches of strangers. Met with jeers, I claw past the people, out onto the ramp, up several flights of stairs and into the night, where I run manically down the street, gasping.

Several attempts to plunge a single coin into a telephone booth are met with disappointing backfires, scraping the sides of the slot but never really sliding in. The small enclosure of the booth all around my feet is littered with dimes. I pull the door closed to stop them from rolling out onto the sidewalk, because I realize this uncomplicated procedure might actually take me some time yet and I may need to conserve coins for consecutive second-tries.

But triumph in this matter utterly eludes me.

Having uncompromisingly failed in getting a single dime into the machine, I stagger off toward Pill's Haberdashery, nearly falling into the place as my full bodily weight pushes into the swinging door. It's only eleven-thirty, but it's already a packed house due to the lunch-time rush. Most of the faces comprise the same old crowd, but it's eerily foreign right now. I feel as if I'm a stranger. Like I don't belong. Everyone looks, somehow, more human than me. Or more accurately, more human than I feel.

Trying my best to keep composed while I flatten out some crumpled bills, I manage to push several of them toward Old Arnold, who is looking me over like I've just escaped from a hospital. 'You alright, Oliver?' he asks, legitimately concerned. 'You look a little pale, son.'

I am unable to come up with anything good. So I settle with telling him my girlfriend is dead.

He blanches, lowering his head. 'Sorry, kiddo,' he offers earnestly, pushing back the hopelessly crumpled money I've given him. 'This one's on the house,' he says.

And it's the first drink I've had in God knows how long. Old Arnold's poured it stronger than usual and after the first sip I thank him for it, falling into a stool at the bar, heaving a sigh of relief that washes over my entire body. The sweat on my brow and down my spine is like ice water, but nonetheless warms me as my body regains some of the heat it was naturally meant to harbor.

There are framed ties on the wall. A pleated pair of dark olive green silk slacks hangs from a frame over a pool table. I listen to balls slap against each other, cracking over the sounds of laughter and camaraderie. All around me, deep voices bitch about jobs, about wives. Laughter tunnels through the room. People cheer. Glasses clink and I hear people yell out for Old Arnold to set up another round.

The smoke is blanket thick and I am thankful that after a few minutes of it I cannot see too far ahead of me. And wide awake, I down the whole glass quickly and shout out into the faceless mix of the noise and chatter for Old Arnold to set up another.

Fumbling with the key to Alice's place, it's nearly half an hour before I am relieved of the racket by a cab pulling up into the driveway. Alice steps out of the car. I nearly crumble to the ground, unsure of my footing. Half-heartedly, I imagine that if I stay still she might pass me by and not notice I'm standing here sweating, unable to manage unlocking the door without assistance.

But the moment she steps out of the cab, indeed the very moment her foot touches the drive port, her head turns in my direction. She comes to me, crouching down, wrapping her arms around me. She calls me Baby, over and over. Her black hair falls in my face, obscuring my vision.

'Oh Oliver, will you please tell me what is the matter with you?'

Pyramids sits down next to Alice, panting, leaning in to lick at my arms only from a cautionary distance. Snow falls from the sky in heavenly drifts, littering us with white dots, making ice of my tears.

The clocks tolls above the mantle. By the fire, I am unable to let go of her.

We listen to music on the stereo and she holds me, all night. She kisses my forehead. I am curled up into a ball, letting her hold me but unable to hold her back. Not even expecting it, when she kisses me I picture in my head a truck-sized jellyfish wrapping me in poison tentacles. But rather than disappearing like it should, changing into something else hideous before clearing to show my beautiful Alice's face once more, the image of the jellyfish instead grows bigger. Its bulbous head lights up with electrical charges and it has fangs that sink into my head as stingers plunge deep into my skin. Waving good-bye, there are sharks shooting away into the darkness of the black water, unlit by the vast head of the jellyfish.

Alice sighs, deeply. When she gets up off the couch, the minute distance between her last touch and my shoulders feels like a void so immense in size I actually lose my hearing and can't tell where in the house she's headed, or even where it is the couch is situated, anymore. I watch her disappear into the darkness of what I think may be the kitchen, thinking she's been swallowed, eaten away from me.

I am terrified.

Softly, to myself, I whisper 'Please don't leave me.'

The words linger at my lips, becoming trails of smoke. Suddenly, Alice appears from the uselessly bright-lit kitchen, making her way toward me. I feel utterly worthless, but somehow stand up straight. 'What did you say? she asks, holding me, wiping sweat from my forehead with a cold cloth.

'Let's go see a movie, Alice.'

No, Oliver. You said something. What was it? Will you tell me what is the matter?'

But I don't know what to say to her and I do not know how to react. *Please, don't leave me*, I want to say to her.

Searching for something, anything. Automatically I think of the dream I had, launching myself over miles and mile of prisons. And I have an idea, but I'm not sure if it's really an idea. 'Let's get out of here,' I say, sounding what I think somebody strong or determined might sound like.

It's good enough, I think.

But when I wake up, jerked violently from sleep, I'm sitting in a non-descript hall, littered with huge oak benches. The sound of my feet stomping the tile underneath me when I shoot my legs out fills the hall with a half-assed reverberation. The sheer pathetic value of the echo as it dies off after just two stomps feels like reality. I think we're at the train station. The train chugging out of the dock is headed toward Pellborough.

Staring at the lit window, the heads all look like mannequins. Just useless figures seated into the train, giving the impression of a long good-bye. Without taking in my surroundings, I get up and walk past the people in the benches, feeling good for some reason. Then a smirk crosses my face, because I am dreaming this train station. The smirk is a lie. It's telling me that the dream is kidding. And I will have to wake up to something horrible. I look around for Alice, but of course she would not be here, would she? Are we at her house? I hope so.

When I wake up, I'm sitting alone in a booth, in a bar. Alice is not here with me. Something happened at her house. I know it. And I passed out. My body broke and I passed out. She isn't here with me. And why should she be? Why would we be here, of all places?

A muted trumpet croons from the jukebox. Smoke stings my eyes. My skin is crawling with distaste and disappointment in myself. Think, think, think. Fuck. What did I do?

Lodged in next to me, there is another sleeping me. A new restlessly dozing Oliver, disheveled and lost in sweet sighs. For the first time since this started happening, I remain entirely calm and I stare at his exposed face, reaching out to touch it, feeling it waxen yet warm and alive. My fingers touch his cheek and his stubble is rough, like mine is. Suddenly, I dig my fingers into his eyes. But still he does not move. My thumbs plunge past the eyeballs, the terrible sound of tight suction charges at my stomach, until I can no longer see the knuckles of my thumbs.

The duplicate me does not move as I grasp the inside of his skull. Blood does not come from his gouged eyes. He sleeps soundly.

I pull my hands away, silenced. From my vicious probing his eyeballs lay open and appear slightly dislodged, as if he were a dummy and his parts were temporarily knocked out of order. Yet still his chest rises and falls, fast asleep with open, fucked-up eyes. Mocking me. Sleeping. Forever.

Forever.

A thin trickle of blood starts to run out from one of the sleeper's sockets.

I look down at my fingers. Half of them are red. Folding these bloodied hands in my lap underneath the table, I lower my head and sigh. A deep tremble rises within me. The sleeping figure next to me nudges against my arm as he breathes away, lost in sleep. It feels like a whole day passes before I finally lift my head again.

There, across from me, is another me.

But this one is different. He is different this time. And what's different about him makes all the difference in the world right now. This one: *He's not sleeping.*

It's me how I am, now. Me awake.

At all once, my skin is dry as paper and as thin. My lips crack and they peel back in revulsion. Oliver is sitting across from me, mouth slightly agape, hunched back against the booth, staring at me with eyes wide in terror. I try to move, to reach for him, but I am frozen in the exact same position as he is, the both of us staring at each other.

I can't even move my mouth. I am trapped.

We sit still, facing each other for quite a long length of time as the muted trumpet continues to blare from the speakers, unconcerned. Oliver sits across from me, slowly and very carefully moving his hands to grip the table at the edge of the booth. Could I talk to him? Would he respond to me? With a sudden feverish move, he shoves the table into my stomach, unleashing a storm of nausea that stays put somehow inside my throat, roiling and falling back down, enclosed in the capsule of my belly, thunderous waves lapping over themselves. The table prods me, but my body is too stiff to be jolted until Oliver finally shoves the table hard, as far as it will go, making it dig into my stomach as it pins my arms where they already dangle uselessly, doubly immovable behind the constraints of the heavy wood.

Shrinking back against the booth, he says nothing, spilling his drink over and darting off. What feels like an eternity proves mere seconds as I build enough energy to *push* the fucking table away. But Oliver is fast. As I begin to give chase, Oliver's already at the door. Out on the street, the sun shines down like a spotlight, penetrating my eyes with a vigorous repeated slashing. I catch the back of his head turning a corner and race toward the end of the block after him. Pushing past endless people who shuffle aimlessly around the sidewalk like scheduled pawns, I round the corner and catch a mere glimpse of Oliver turning another corner, just a block ahead.

The alley is thin, littered with trash from the two restaurants on either side. The other me – the one who woke up *before I did* this time – is climbing over a dumpster and hopping the tall boarded fence.

With a sharp, razorblade yearning scouring the insides of my veins as blood rushes, I chase him, still coughing from the blow of the table, pulsating, gasping, sweating feverishly as I pitch endlessly forward, under and past the great tree with its branches spread out in a dark cloud. But always I am rewarded for my speed with merely a fleeting and haunting glimpse of the back of Oliver's head, the crook of his elbow or the heel of his shoe. Always, he is one corner ahead of me.

I pursue him for blocks. He eludes me for miles.

Over fences, through courtyards and plazas, small thickets and empty streets. Long before the sun began to set, I started to notice the buildings we have been weaving through were no longer familiar to me. I let it go, not caring where I was or where we would end up, so long as I *caught* Oliver and held him up to my face and asked him what...

...and what? What would I ask him? Myself. What would I ask myself if I caught him?

He flew over the hood of a car just as I crawled up the steps of a project basement we shot through. His body disappears over the car. When I finally reach it, I am able to catch just the back of his head, loose curls hanging in the wind as he shoots around the corner of yet another unfamiliar building.

My feet are so ravaged I am bleeding through the shoes. The heart inside my skeleton's chest pumps forcibly, covering the fading footfalls of the other Oliver.

With every last ounce of blood propelling me, I give chase.

Sometimes I stop to catch my breath, but it's not possible to really do so and so relentlessly I recommence, harder and harder until it feels the bones in my legs may splinter at any moment.

And *always*, with each constant turn, my arrival is just close enough to seize some mockingly infuriating glimpse of the back of Oliver's head – *my head* – as it rounds yet another corner, loops around *another* building.

I keep running, because I must find myself.

My feet pound the sidewalk with as much control, as much solidity and as much permanence, as the falling rain.

worry,
but then it's time
for sleep

The room drifted into a very slow, exhaled focus, but nothing of release carried in the feeling that crawled its way from the muddy smog in his head, down his body to the torso that felt too heavy and the legs underneath just barely supporting him. 'Where'd that doctor go?' he mumbled. Amidst an otherwise dead silence, his voice rang intrusively loud in the stone hall at the darker end of the cafeteria's dining room, itself a bleak cave entrance far off from the people who'd already secured their meals, sitting down at the tables in small groups of two or three, without any words being exchanged between their soft, silent bites of sandwiches and lifeless sips from soup spoons.

Everyone in the dining hall looked blank and lifeless, unable to find their focus. Hospitals are cold places.

In this silence, the man's voice bounced off undecorated white painted stone walls, moving perspiring soda machines to hum louder in order to catch up to the useless calamity that interrupted everything that wasn't happening. He looked over toward a small woman who hobbled with great effort across a sparkling white floor to a salad bar close to the registers. And he called to her.

'Is the doctor dead?'

But the sluggish, hunched-over woman didn't answer. Nor did she seem even to hear him at all, though a few of those in the dining hall looked up from their cold soup bowls to give him the once over before disappearing from the now, painfully dragging spoons up to their lips, again. Fluorescent lights over the table were so bright he could see glares fragmenting off spoon handles, twinkling like a night sky, here in this cold, lonely cafeteria with no windows.

He couldn't move his arms.

Or what passed for arms, after surgery.

A nurse with strawberry colored hair, wearing a familiar, if peculiar, hospital smile on her face stood then in front of him, blocking his view of the wasteland in the dining room, offering her outstretched hand, palm down, ladylike and demure. Not quite a handshake, yet not reasonably dissimilar. He tried to raise a hand to grasp hers to complete this shake, but his arms felt like pins, needles, parasites, and boiling water. Maybe it was the drugs wearing off, but his body felt like a nerve rebellion, avoiding proper calls for action. Her face grew deep red and she blinked horribly, pulling her hand back to her side, coughing into a closed fist, searching for the right mode to fall back into. Her embarrassment carried the scent of fresh-cut flowers and he found it hard to understand what was happening when she grasped, instead, his shoulder. Smiling, not entirely reassuring even though her touch shocked him into a somewhat decently effected state of ease. Either a trick of the natural nurse or the end of the world.

In a practiced but charmingly songlike voice, she asked him 'Would you like some help seeing you to an available table in the dining room, Mr. Cavalry?'

'No,' he answered abruptly, unsure if this was actually the case, his voice raspy but not entirely lost. Then 'I don't think I can eat right now, really.'

'Of course, Mr. Cavalry. That's understandable.' She beamed a perfectly considerate smile, bright white teeth and red lips. It took a second, but she finished it off with the friendly nod nurses must have to rehearse in sick-room mirrors before rustling the almost dead from almost last sleeps.

Very lightly, almost non-existent, angelically soothing violin strains whispered across the cold cafeteria from overhead speakers in the ceiling that were distributed all throughout the expansive, wasteland-lonely room. The longer he directed his attentions to it, the more he started to feel like he was in another world – or at least any place but the hospital. But then the nurse spoke again and it broke his concentration.

'My name is Helen, as it were. Everyone calls me Nurse Helen. You do remember me, don't you, Mr. Cavalry?'

Of course he did. From after he'd been administered the proper amounts of anesthetics, as the room had filled up with doctors in blue and the brilliant overhead fluorescents blinked on in patches up above him, flooding his vision with white, flooding his head up like a dream you simply can't wring yourself from.

Before he'd entirely drowned in that – what felt like mud in his head – drifting off into a painless nap the medicine urged on to ease his body into quiet submission before the operation had begun, he'd been introduced to Nurse Helen by one of the friendlier doctors. She'd smiled so reassuringly, said Hello, and put her face mask on over the studied bun of her hair, nestling it over nose and mouth like a bubble. He'd known she was still smiling under the surgical mask, because of the way her eyes had squinted as she tilted her head just a bit in his direction.

This was the same nurse, here now, who'd been there for him then. Nurse Helen in the cafeteria.

'How are your arms feeling this morning, Mr. Cavalry?'

Dazed, slow, not wanting to look down at his strange-fitting arms, he sighed. The way she said his name sounded harsh in the essential emptiness of resonance around them, as though he were trapped somewhere, being spoken to through a tube or an intercom. 'Please, he said, trying to raise his hand in protest, but giving up. 'Please call me Alain.'

With a hand on his shoulder, more inward the base of his neck, warm and friendly, almost seductively if this hadn't been the single most uncomfortable moment of his life, she smiled again. And it was a nice smile, though she wouldn't touch the end of his shoulder or look down at his arms.

He did, though.

Alain looked down at his arms – the ones she would neither touch nor visually acknowledge – blankly letting it soak into his vision.

It was hard to look at and he was groggy, at best, but it was just plain hard.

The doctor had removed the unsalvageable remains of the grasping limbs he'd grown and lived thirty-eight years with, taking them off, each of them, at the shoulder. Those arms that had been, they were now replaced with octopus tentacles.

He tried as best he could, but could not get these new limbs – the tentacles – to move. Searching first through memory and then through random bodily spasms for the nerves in these arms, for any sort of feeling that felt like fingers, or a hand, to his horror, the shriveling spherical suction cups near the curling tips of the tentacles flared and contracted.

Alain winced.

Nurse Helen squeezed his shoulder a little tighter, so reassuringly. 'It may take some time, Mr. Cavalry...I'm sorry . . . *Alain*...But before long, you'll find movement will return to you at a productive, *natural* rate. We'll be here for you while and until you fully rehabilitate the use of muscle movement. So whenever you need me,' her voice more songlike than ever, like a radio broadcast from a crackling bygone era, hollow and haunting, 'just call my name.'

It was only now that she glanced so very fleetingly down to the soft gray tentacles dangling lifelessly from the sleeves of his spotted gray hospital gown, blinking surreptitiously. Then she looked back into his eyes with a wide, close-mouthed expression chiseled over her face that was both friendly and reassuring as well as trustworthy – that nurse thing, the perfect response played out both by those who could and couldn't pass it off. But behind it, maybe in that slight twinkle in the eyes after she finished speaking, there was some phantom piece of worry escaping from somewhere behind all that night-class-learned surety, a glossy forefront of a look that promises but doesn't quite physically come through in the end.

'However, it's extremely important that we keep them wet, Alain. Perhaps we should go back to the emergency room now and have the doctor submerse them in water while we wait for your appetite to return.' She started to lead the way out of the cafeteria, offering her hand again, ahead of them, for him to make the first step.

He nodded, slowly, looking off toward a few dozen people with their heads down who were slowly and barely eating up grim lunches at the tables in the dining room, with their fingers curled around the handles of cold ceramic coffee cups. Lifting steamless black drinks to their lips. Cutting small bits of food with forks and knives. Stirring cold soup. None of it penetrating severe sedation.

'Okay, Nurse Helen,' Alain breathed very quietly, still watching the people in the dining hall who all had their heads down, some of them possibly thinking about their various somebodies up above in one of the many frosty hospital rooms, hooked to blinking, beeping machines, heart rates shifting throughout the day and night.

He tried to move his tentacles around, again. All he received in response were more flared suction cups.